THE FINE LINE

Emily Chesshire Thompson

WestBow Press books may be ordered through booksellers or by contacting:

WestBow Press
A Division of Thomas Nelson
1663 Liberty Drive
Bloomington, IN 47403
www.westbowpress.com
1-(866) 928-1240

ISBN: 978-1-4497-7394-6 (sc)
ISBN: 978-1-4497-7395-3 (hc)
ISBN: 978-1-4497-7393-9 (e)

Library of Congress Control Number: 2013901772

Printed in the United States of America

WestBow Press rev. date: 2/19/2013

For Rick, my encourager and biggest fan,
I can't stop loving you.

Acknowledgements

Sometimes we hear a faint whisper that calls us something more than our name. Sometimes that same faint whisper speaks aloud a calling that others have noticed along the way. Sometimes it is only obedience that turns those whispers to shouts, that takes a woman and turns her into an author, that takes passion and turns it into reality, that takes a soul and turns it into a Follower.

"the Spirit whispered" Acts 10:19, The Message

My journey of faith has resulted in writing my first novel, a journey that was highly influenced by wonderful women that the Lord placed in my life. I thank each of you for guiding, mentoring, and pouring into me. I feel so incredibly blessed for the time I've had with each one of you. May women continue encouraging one another as we follow Christ.

Gina Allison, thank you for grabbing ahold of this lost girl, loving me, and introducing me to God's Word. **Jaime Wolter**, thank you for discipling me and never giving up! **Jen Duey**, thank you for being a Godly friend and walking alongside me. **Teresa Tate**, thank you for being an example of placing God first, for teaching me to set high standards and never compromise. **Trisha Porter**, thank you for teaching me to pray for my husband and for embracing us. **Debbie Newman**, thank you for showering me with God's love and showing me that raising amazing kids is possible! **Ida Soto**, thank you for prayer, for passing on prayer, for always encouraging us. **Angela Taylor**, thank you for the woman you've become. **Buffi Crump**, thank you for speaking God's words and ways without apology. **Kay Dalke**, thank you for generously sharing parts of your journey and encouraging mine. **Kathryn Swadley**, thank you for being an example of loving the unlovely. **Marzia Castro**, thank you for opening your home and heart to me. For sharing your family and faith, for every minute I had with you, I am grateful. I miss you beyond words.

This novel would not have been complete without input from amazing individuals. To each of you, I treasure you and consider it a privilege to have your names included in my first novel. To **Kathryn Swadley**, *contributing editor*, thank you for being the first to read my work cover to cover. Your opinion and input was honest, real, and invaluable. Your attention to detail and the overall storyline was just what I needed to continue. To **Vicki Wade**, *contributing editor*, thank you for detailed input and speaking about these characters as though they were real. I knew I had done my job! To **Kay Dalke**, thank you for reading this in the raw, initial phases. Your thoughts helped me aim more clearly and stay on target. To **Susan Marsh-Narigon**, thank you for seeing something special in me and for encouraging me to pursue it. I believed in myself because you believed in me. Thank you for loving me beyond the classroom.

As you read these pages, may each of you grasp the fine line and determine if it should remain or be redefined.

THE FINE LINE

Prologue

IT'S WHAT DIVIDED ME FROM them. It was the door that allowed me to pass freely and the door that kept them bound. It was everything I never imagined existing in this world.

"Para los servicios religiosos." The bars gently opened, guided by the hand of a guard. He reeked of his own indecency, the way he leaned over and casually pursued his job, as if every visitor belonged in a grand heap of nothing along with the nothings we came to visit. The authority of his thin, black uniform had a sickening effect on his attitude and a sickening effect on me. He wore his uniform like armor. They all wore them like armor. I scanned the guards briefly as this one began his tedious routine. His large ink stamp licked the inner side of my left arm. I blew the dark ink dry and flung my borrowed bags to the counter. The counter separated the guards and I, the only real separation I would desire in this place. They barely looked through my bag, never really caring. Never really suspecting that my innocent face could conceive of committing a crime.

I stepped through the familiar closet door into the little barren room where she sat. She shamelessly looked me up and down, beneath the bounds of my bra, through the creases in my pockets, to my panties. She filed her nails away; she filed her life away; she filed me in as number 32.

Number 32. The small square of white paper fit snuggly in my back pocket. Another day. I waited as Marco took a bit longer to be searched today. They were even less inquisitive with him. His guitar case was always opened with a hint of nonchalance. The guitar itself admired for a moment, then just simply handed to him. No glimpse inside or a pat down, just another easy-access day.

It was rare that I finished first. The men coming in were far fewer than the women. Their motives were less obvious than the fancied-up females waiting for a reaction from their man or any man for that matter. The women who frequented the grounds were detectable. They knew the routine. Their stomachs prompted them to bathe in perfume to mask the odorous air, and their faces knew smiling at one another showed weakness, vulnerability, emotion perhaps. Emotionless were those women who cared not if their men became free but only if the walls remained open to ease their insecurities. The security that life on the inside didn't have to merge with life on the outside. The security that their man was faithful this time around. Most of all, the security of always being wanted, needed, longed for. This was, of course, the place for that. A thousand Hispanic men bumping into a thousand Hispanic men. The thrill of a tight pair of brightly colored jeans hugging the thighs of any female was enough to send them out of their cages and into the squelching heat.

I glanced at the others who chose to spend their Wednesday morning in such a place as this, curious of their intentions. Wives? Girlfriends? Sisters, perhaps? Marco smiled at each guard as he came out of the little room, not fazed by the search. For him it had been years of this old routine: the walls, the guards, the numbers, the ink stamps, dirt sweeping into your eyes with a simple shift in the wind, the black entrance, and all that awaited on the other side. For me, this was anything but routine.

Marco gently raised his eyebrows and nodded toward the dry dirt before us. He wore a simple straw sombrero to block the heat we would all be dodging in just a few blistering hours.

A beaten path of dirt and slivers of weeds led to a solid black wall, as tall and thick as they come. A glassy-eyed guard flipped the circumference of my wrist to reveal the inkblot on the other side. I felt for my number in my back left pocket one more time, making sure I could exit. As the guard opened the thickest black door, I stepped one single step through.

Men sat in grass, in dirt, against a tree. One after another – everywhere I looked. Shoeless, shirtless, tanks, t-shirts, well-posed, humped-over. I stepped around them, trying to follow the lead of an unfamiliar face, a mere boy. The boy's smile calmed all but my eyes, which never ceased to absorb this place. I heard conversations, even joined in, but the images forever clouded my eyes. Images of hope attached to desperation. Smiles connected to lost eyes, eyes looking frantically for eyes to meet theirs, to pause, to connect. Souls starving to be accepted, to be functional, to have a purpose for this day, this moment, this life.

The men swarmed to help us carry anything. And everything. A moment to do something with nothing. Grabbing. Reaching. Touching. Greeting. Smiling. Offering. Marco casually motioned for them to give us space as he lovingly patted a back, put his arm around a familiar shoulder, and smiled no differently than in his own home. He briefly glanced in my direction before heading forward with a few new faces. His demeanor instantly put me at ease, and I walked a few feet behind him, absorbing this side of the wall. I followed them as they followed the pathways formed by a chain link fence, guards scarcely present.

And that's how it happened. I missed the fine line. The line that defines right from wrong, worthy from unworthy, clean from dirty, the loved from the unlovable, the every day Jane from the branded criminal. It was the line that all others saw the moment the black door opened. And the line that I somehow missed.

1

a wednesday in may

MY TRIP TO NORTHERN MEXICO began as a quick fix to a messed up relationship. Marco had opened his doors to me. I took him up on the offer and planned on visiting his family for a week to soak up wisdom from a fatherly figure, leave my life for a brief moment, and come home refreshed. It was God's timing, providing me with a moment apart from the world that had caved in around me. Ever since I first visited Mexico, it warmed my heart, so it was an easy "yes" when the phone rang. My fourth day in Mexico, I found myself here. In a prison. On a Wednesday. In May.

More than the norm gathered that day, my day one. Gathered perhaps to see blue eyes on top of a smiling face. Or to find a moment of shade and song in a world that ached for both. Whatever the reason, we were there, and they were there.

I follow Marco along the barren path, among the many men, to a small cement-walled shelter in the middle of the grounds. He smiles, I smile. He hugs, I hug. He offers a hand, I offer a hand. They lean in for my cheek, I lean in for theirs.

As my fingers twist caps off liters of Coke and my hands pour drinks for them, my eyes immediately see into them, as if their skin is transparent, exposing their very souls. A young kid, maybe fourteen, circulates and says his hellos with smiles stretching his cheeks back out, cheeks that have gone far too long without exercise. Older men sit, skeptical but grateful for the luxury of a Coke. Most gravitate toward Marco, each wanting a moment to say hello. He never forces a single smile, never a slight roll of the eye. He gleams like Santa Claus might if he could see the reaction of each child on Christmas morning, yet he bears no gifts. Just a slight belly. I continue capturing pictures in my mind until my ears hear the first English syllables floating about.

"Pedro." A guy offers me his hand, a relief after so many have leaned in for my cheek. His black hair is pulled back, strands around his face too short to stay back shade his darkened face.

"Hi, I'm Maggie," I say. "Finally! Someone speaks English!" I reach out my hand, relieved I won't have to stumble through the day with my limited Spanish.

"Yeah, I used to live in Kansas. I went to school there and played football." Pedro's accent flows from each word, but I will soon find out there isn't much that will interfere with Pedro if he has his mind set on communicating.

"Thank goodness! Maybe you can fill me in on all the conversation I'm missing." I smile, just like always, wondering why it feels no different, why talking to a prisoner in a prison feels no different at all.

"Oh this stuff? Don't worry about that, boring hellos, how are yous. We're in here, right? It's not like there's a whole lot we've been up to. What about you? Did you just come to visit today?"

Something about his question stays with me. It's the absence of expectation. Another one-timer who will fill this day but no others.

"Yeah," I say, "Marco first told me about you guys when I met him on a mission trip a couple of years ago, and I'm visiting his family this week, so he asked me to come with him today." Just as I begin to smile, he leans in to my space.

"Your eyes are beautiful. So blue." I just smile. Something so every day keeps my words from coming out. He's just like any other guy. Isn't this place supposed to be some oversized awful container with all the nobodies of society? Didn't I just meet someone that isn't allowed the freedoms we all are? And yet, he brushes his stray hairs back to reveal the darkest black eyes, and I could fall right into them.

"Are you okay?" He asks, "We're not scaring you, are we?" Each word sounds just a little better sprinkled with his accent.

"No, not at all. For some reason, I'm not scared at all," I tease. "Guess I'm just quiet since I don't know anyone."

And there we go. Pedro introduces me to the entire room within minutes. I follow him, nodding like I have a clue when they say more than the recognizable frequency phrases I have memorized. Such a blend of society here in this place: old and young, well-dressed and filthy, clean-cut and overgrown, fingers smooth to the touch, fingers made of hardened calluses. Accompanied by the smooth strums of Marco's guitar, my mind captures pictures like a photographer clicking hundreds of times, afraid to miss a single moment of the action.

While others sing, I watch. Some men sing along with Marco, knowing each and every word. A few just close their eyes and move to the rhythm, thankful for moments of peace. Uncomfortable faces look around the circle, drawn to the sound of live music, not yet thirsty for worship. Some stop in only to take a glance at me. Others grab a free cup of Coke and leave. But I do nothing of the sort. I just see into them; I can't help but see into them. My eyes close in an attempt to figure out the Spanish words they sing. My heart, however, sings a song of another kind.

Lord, why am I here? What am I doing in this place? Kansas? He was playing football in Kansas, and now he's here? Oh, God, it's so much to take in. Let me love them, Lord. Teach me to love them like You do. Just fill me with love. Use me, I pray. How precious they are. They sing like they love you with everything in them. Thank you for bringing me here, for every moment today.

I open my eyes to a mixture of grown men sweating, most undeodorized, and voices yelling rather than harmonizing. Yet, in the midst of this seemingly chaotic choir is the presence of the Almighty God. A presence so undeniable I begin to regret all the times I was so preoccupied with singing perfectly back home that I missed out on worship itself. Here He is, in this place. In a prison. On a Wednesday. In May.

My eyes focus on the stranger across from me. Shining like a child sitting with the biggest lollypop imaginable, he just smiles away. Of course, he isn't a child; he's typical for this kind of place. Tattooed with pictures of every sort: women, dragons, a mix-match of patterns, knives, and cartoons. A bit of everything is painted on that skinny mural of his. He swings his feet from the old folding table to the tune of the guitar that Marco strums. His grungy Nikes are half white, half black, half-dirty, half-clean. Sweat drips down his colorful arms. His harsh features soften with the peaceful swaying of his feet. Hair chopped over the ears reaches past his shoulders in the back, complementing the once bright blue wife beater he wears. He perfectly fits the image of a prisoner, yet sings as though he's completely free. Photo after photo continues to be captured in my mind as worship ends. Worship. My day one.

I glance around our circle, fifteen men, Marco, me. The men don't have Bibles, pens, or journals. They're here with nothing at all. It doesn't take long to realize that the absence of supplies has nothing to do with the presence of desire. Marco takes out his Bible and begins explaining a new study, reading the book of Ephesians together. His details are way beyond my simple Spanish, but I can follow well enough. With that, I grab my Bible out of my little backpack and glance at Marco's page every now and then to make sure I have my verses straight.

As the study begins, I try to stay focused on God's Word, knowing that Marco's purpose here is to study the Bible with these men, to increase their understanding of the freedom they have in Christ. But as hard as I try, I find myself distracted, not only by the huge language barrier, but also by the newness of it all.

Just last week I was planning a fun-filled summer. Now I'm sitting in a circle with prisoners, finding it necessary to remember that they are, in fact, prisoners. Somehow this place, small cement buildings, chain-link fences, dorm-like buildings, and shades of brown roaming in every direction, feels comfortable. A community of sorts. Not the awful place I imagine when I hear the word prison. Well, not yet.

Interrupting my thoughts, Pedro's fingers slide the corner of my page to the left. Quietly, he points to Ephesians 1:19. I read a once familiar verse with new eyes. "I also pray that you will understand the incredible greatness of God's power for us who believe him. This is the same mighty power that raised Christ from the dead..."

Suddenly the smallest words take on a whole new meaning. You. Us. Pray that these men will understand the incredible greatness of God's power. Somehow I'm supposed to believe that in here without a mother, father, wife, friend, stripped of all luxuries and some necessities, I'm supposed to pray for these men to understand the incredible greatness of God's power? How are they possibly going to see God's power? Forget about understanding justice, wrath, compassion, second chances, or forgiveness. Ephesians brings us to the incredible greatness of God's power. Us. Not the small town girl in her affluent neighborhood and all her friends, not the college Bible study group, or the ones who have always walked the straight and narrow. Us is now this atypical circle of men, far from any circle I've ever been a part of. Bible study. My day one.

Before I know it, a loud air horn fills the air and nearly sends me flat on the ground. I jump so far that a few laugh. All of the guys instantly stand up from their seats in the dirt, on the folding table, and against the wall to move to the open doorway. Within seconds, Marco and I are alone in this roofless cement building.

I watch the young kid I saw earlier make his way out the doorway and ask, "Who's that?"

"The kid? That's Maelo. He's sixteen. Let's see, I think he came last summer, maybe last fall. He's been here about a year, I think." Marco describes him in terms of time.

"Do you know why he's here? He seems so young to be mixed in with all these men!" I look right at Marco for some sort of guidance, an explanation of some sort. Really? Sixteen? It scares me to think of what he's been through in here. He's the cutest thing, not even a hair on his face to shave.

Another air horn blares and sends my hands to cover my ears. Marco waits a minute before answering me, "Maggie, I believe Maelo is in here for something pretty bad. You might learn this one day. Give it time. For now, love on him. Be Christ in front of him. Love them first, learn what they've done if the Lord leads you to, but let's not start off with that." His words make sense, but they don't do anything for my curiosity.

Several more air horns blare over the next few minutes, and Marco tells me that there's a two o'clock bed check every day. They have ten blares, one every minute, a countdown to get inside their cells. They are counted, documented, and released at two thirty. The same routine every day.

"What do you usually do while they're gone?" I ask, ready for the next adventure.

"Well, sweet Maggie, this old man usually lays right here on this old table and relaxes, taking in the sky." Marco sits on the folding table and pats the space next to him, inviting me to join him.

We sit in complete silence for the next thirty minutes, never once looking at each other. We simply take in the sway of the clouds, the breezeless day, and the disgustingly awful smell that I've only known before in small doses. The smell of rotted food that meets the sun, bakes for days, and seeps out of the garbage can as you throw in the next trash bag. Here, that smell permeates the air. There is no lid, no escape.

Despite the smell, I can't help but smile as I think about the men. Pictures of this morning scroll through my mind: Antonio's tattoo mural, a pink polo man whose arms were without an ink stamp, the mounds of men sitting throughout the path, a man shoving his tweety bird keychain in my face, this dilapidated cement building that has hints of turquoise paint clinging to it, Maelo's dimples showing when I said hello, a shirtless guy with every rib showing leaning against the wall for the entire Bible study. Scrolling and scrolling.

Pretty soon, my mind is interrupted when Antonio comes running in the doorway of the cemented shelter, ready to get started. His scratchy voice greets me, "Mayhee" without a hint of a "g" anywhere. I smile at this newfound way to say my name. He goes straight for Marco's guitar, takes it out of its case as though it's his own, and sits on the ground. I can't help but smile. Watching Antonio is like watching a little boy play with a new toy. He's so excited, so filled with energy. Without a musical inkling, he strums away.

Guys come back in, one after the other. A few new faces peek through the open doorway and stay there, not ready to take a full step into this world of worship and Bible study. The room takes just a few minutes to fill up, ears ready to hear Marco read and pause to explain, sometimes standing in excitement, sometimes pulling up a guy or two to bring the Word to life. I love watching Marco here. It's a lot different than the Marco I first met interpreting for teams of American teenagers on mission trips. Although always full of energy, there's something so fatherly about watching him with these men. It's his ability to embrace them, challenge them, guide them. There's something deep within Marco that draws them in and brings out smiles and laughter. Even the most somber faces I see tend to let a smile slip here and there.

After getting through the first two chapters of Ephesians, one of the more serious faces moves from his spot on the wall and takes a step toward Marco. He gets the attention of the entire room. Clearly a man who usually holds back, I have to know what he's saying.

"Marco, what did he say?" I ask.

"Alan asked why God didn't do something to change his life, his circumstances, to help him avoid some of the decisions he made." Marco continues to translate as the men all begin opening up.

"And Jorge just said that he doesn't have that question, but he wonders if God is so powerful, how is it he lets terrible things happen." Marco explains, now giving a name to the man in the pink polo.

Pedro comments first in Spanish, then translates for me, "Jorge, God gave us free will. He didn't make us robotic; he didn't make choices for us. Evil makes terrible things happen. People's evil decisions; People have evil ideas; there's evil within a person." With that, Jorge, with his clean-shaven face and perfectly buzzed hair, lifts his chin toward Marco, as if requesting his response.

"Pedro's right. We all have free will, Jorge. We make our own decisions. That's why we must follow Christ and learn a new way of living after this life has taught us a wrong way." Jorge's eyes are locked on Marco, clearly valuing his every word.

"And Alan, I understand. A God who is all-powerful, as we talked about last week, that God would seem to be able to do anything, fix anything, but remember that if He interferes with our decisions, that takes away our choice. Friends, we can get over hurt and work through our pain, but most important today is understanding that God did not cause your pain." Pedro's words echo Marco's explanations to the men.

With that, Pedro continues to translate Marco's every word for me until the closing prayer begins. As I listen in darkness, I hear more than one voice leading men in prayer. I hear voices echoing Marco's words, voices creating prayers of their own, soft mumbles of a simple, "Gracias a Dios" all at once. One room full of many prayers.

As the men stop praying, my heart begins feeling a depth unlike any other. A depth soon interrupted by a daily deadline, the five o'clock departure.

"Is it five o'clock already?" I can hardly believe it's over.

"Say your goodbyes, Maggie. We've got to go." Simple words, hard orders. Say goodbye? I stare at my black pants and the pink beads hanging from my necklace. Goodbye? My throat instantly gets a lump in it, and I feel my eyes turn against me and fill up with tears. Seeing me cry cannot be the last thing these guys remember.

Pedro leans in close to me, "What's for dinner, Maggie?" He breaks my ache with a little humor.

"Dinner?" I laugh. I wipe my eyes and smile at his perfect smile, "Well, dinner wasn't exactly on my mind, but I imagine popcorn, like the last three nights."

"Well, you enjoy that, dear," his words are bland. "I am glad you came today," Pedro says it as if he needs to convince me. And just that quickly, he leaves, as if that is a sufficient goodbye.

"Pedro," my fingers reach his left arm, "I'm really glad I got to meet you." Our eyes meet and no other words are exchanged, but for the next brief moments, our eyes say what our mouths cannot.

It was more than a casual day with acquaintances. Time has a way of expanding hours in this place, and the mundane has a way of becoming meaningful. It feels different here. Pedro. My day one.

Eyes stare at me as I follow the path of the chain link fence. Eyes that don't care who I am. Eyes that want to be walking with me. Eyes that can't help but undress me. Eyes that ache to step through the door. Eyes that can't remember what would be there if they did step through. Eyes that long for their somebodies to visit. Eyes that reveal life on this side. Eyes that hide all within. Eyes that beg for attention. Eyes that have never known affirmation. Eyes that make most uneasy. Eyes that make me look again.

A guard gives me a nod, requesting the paper I have in my back left pocket. I quickly remove the white square that labels me number 32. With that, the guard uses all his strength to pull open the door that's thicker than his waist and nearly twice his height. Marco and I step one single step through. And it's over that quickly. We're done.

Absorbing it all leaves me overflowing with images, questions, and new thoughts never before taking up space in my mind. I have no real words to say.

Marco waits until we get outside of the prison gates and step on to the rocky parking lot before asking, "What do you think?"

"I'm amazed." His arms draw me in and squeeze me, his sweaty brow moistening my face, "Few can do it, Maggie. Only a few."

And I was one.

One who can cross over the fine line undisturbed. One who can test the bounds and come out untouched. One who can freely pass back and forth. Or so I thought…

2

two days later

I'M SCHEDULED TO LEAVE SATURDAY morning, but find myself attached to Marco's family, in this not-so-American culture, which lacks air conditioning, fast food, a filling dinner, and much more. The thought of packing up and heading back to Iowa for another summer before heading back to college in the fall isn't settling well with me. I know I can't return. School would be fine in August: a new year, a new dorm, a new roommate. But everything back home seems to be overshadowed by a Wednesday in May.

Marco wakes us up on this Friday morning, like each morning, by blaring the stereo with worship music. His daughter Rosie, who just graduated from high school and kindly made room for me in her bedroom, leans over and rolls her eyes as I look up at her from my campout on her bedroom floor. She grabs my hand tight saying, "Oh my gosh, is this normal? He's crazy!" We laugh out loud.

"Normal? No, Rosie, but was there ever a question?" In all my previous encounters with her dad, "normal" was never a word that came to mind. Extreme, hilarious, a bit overly excited at times, but never normal. He has a heart that I wish we all had. Most of all, we have a connection. The kind of connection that only God can be responsible for. He looks at me and asks me questions about the secrets within the secrets that no one could possibly know. We're kindred spirits.

Living, breathing, and following the Word of God and life of Christ does something to a man. Sharing the gospel and mentoring men is his life. He doesn't exist without the Word. He doesn't go a day without it. So, his method of waking the house makes me smile, although I'm sure Rosie would prefer a quieter, more subtle way. In Marco's house, you are going to awaken to praise and worship music, like it or not. I'm thankful for his immense faith. Without it, he wouldn't be able to read me. Without it, I may have never known the feel of a Godly home, even if it was only for a week.

Rosie and I head for the living room and wait for her brothers to emerge. Victor and Diego share bunks in the only other bedroom. Marco and his wife Maria have a bed out in the open in the place most would call a dining room, a tight space that exudes warmth unlike any I have ever known.

Rosie wears her barely-there shorts, a tank top, and her thick, ugly glasses that are stuck together with tape. Mine aren't much better. In fact, there is no way I will put them on in daylight, so I scramble for the sink to put my contacts in. Rosie slips by me to the bathroom. I glance at the missing doorknob to the bathroom door and choose a chair that faces the other direction and wait for the boys to come out. Maria takes breakfast orders: pita bread and cheese or cantaloupe. I don't like eating first thing in the morning, but I know after a week here that along with the afternoon comes the only full meal, and my tummy will be growling all night if I skip food now. "Cantaloupe, por favor."

Marco is carefully ironing his coral shirt, getting ready to make his morning trip to the prison. I can barely think of Marco going. Wednesday has not yet left me. I just replay the pictures my mind so eagerly took. Being here isn't being there, and that's where I want to be. I'm struggling to fight back tears knowing he'll be there in just an hour. I want to jump in that ugly non-air-conditioned Bronco, smell the stench of the sewer, see the hardened guards, get filled with questions, wonder why and who and what, when, how. Just one more time.

Rosie grabs my empty fruit bowl and sets it inside hers, heading for the kitchen. Marco puts his sombrero on and looks around for something. He seems to be asking where something is, but my Spanish is barely here this morning. I can hardly watch him, knowing he will be there, with them, knowing the drive to the prison is only about twenty minutes to the outskirts of town. My eyes have been exposed to the worst of the worst homes in this area. Simple bed sheets acting as roofs, attached to poles in the ground, far worse shelter than anything back in the States. I knew Wednesday that the stench in the air meant this area was reserved for three things: the prison, the poorest of the poor, and the city's landfill. Yet, I want so badly to be a part of that again.

Pedro's question keeps running through my mind: "*Did you just come to visit today?*" Do they know that it wasn't torture, that my one day with them has touched me in a way nothing else ever has? Or do they think I'm grateful to get out of there and go back to my normal life? All I want is to be there with them. In that place. Something is drawing me to the prison with such insistence I can't keep quiet anymore.

"Marco, can I come with you?" I had to ask.

"Right now?"

"I can get ready in five minutes." I'm nearly begging. Something within me knows I need to go.

"Come here." His gentle voice prompts me out of my chair and into the living room seat next to him on the sofa. "Maggie, Maria's taking you shopping today."

"I know, but I'd rather come with you." I fight the tears.

"Only a few can actually come into the prison and deal with it like you did. Love touched them through you, Maggie. You weren't hiding anything behind that smile, which is rare. You have something special God has given you. I see it. They see it, too. Don't cry, Love." He wipes the tears from my left cheek and places his hand on my cheek.

"I was waiting to see if the desire was present in you. I didn't want to give you the idea. I wanted you to decide on your own. You see, I have prayed for months for someone to come with me. There are too many guys coming for me to teach all of them. You could read with them, sing along with us, even teach English. Maria said you are welcome to stay here with us this summer if you would like. The decision is yours." My answer was in the tears that streamed downward in quick succession.

"Ok." Simple but enough.

"Now today, you need to stay. Call home. Get permission. You can help Maria today and shop if you like. You must come to morning prayer at church each morning before we go to the prison. No prayer, no prison. God will refresh us and meet us, and people will pray over us. We walk through the prison gates bathed in prayer, never without. It is God that gives you joy there. Let him fill you first. So today, you stay. Tomorrow, come to prayer with me. And then we'll go." His sweet voice speaks to the place in my soul that longs for just this. I smile and feel his kiss upon my forehead as he makes his rounds of goodbyes before heading out.

I never could've imagined all that was to come. And I never could have imagined how essential the fine line would become.

3

the next day

MY 4:30 WAKE UP CALL was welcomed. I had been lying awake in bed for nearly an hour, anxious for the day to get started. My jeans and t-shirt were laid out on Rosie's miniature dresser. I quickly changed, finger-combed my hair into a ponytail, and rinsed my face in freezing water before sticking my contacts in. Marco was tying his shoes as I headed out the front door. The night sky was completely dark. No streetlights exist here. A cool breeze swept the rest of the night's heat from my skin as my hand reached for the unlocked Bronco door. Just a few more hours...

We ride with the windows up for the first time since my arrival. Usually the leather seats burn to the touch and the broken AC forces the windows open. But it's cool at this hour. Pleasantly cool.

The familiar tent church is different at this hour too. The usual spread of hundreds of folding chairs is gone. The huge wooden stage is without instruments, bare, showing no signs of the few thousand that gather there three times a week for intense worship. The coffeehouse lights are on, and people are walking toward the largest actual building owned by the church, one I have never been in before. I follow Marco. There are no greetings this morning, no smiles or eye contact. Everyone walks with an agenda, ready for prayer to begin.

I find an unoccupied spot in a corner and begin to pray.

Father, thank You. Thank You, Lord, for this opportunity. I need You. I need Your guidance and help here. Father, help me be a witness for You. Oh, Lord. I'm so excited to go again. Please help me channel this energy and work on Your behalf. Lord, please reveal anything to me that I need to repent of, so that I might be a vessel You can use.

I just pray that You would cover each man there with Your angels, Lord. Soften their hearts so they will be open to Your words. I pray You work on them now so they are tender soil, ready to hear Your truth and change their lives. Lord, I saw so much pain in their eyes. Pain that You know perfectly. Pain that You watched them live. Father, give me wisdom to minister to them and say the words they need to hear. Lord, I pray You would bring more men to this ministry, so this prison is full of men living for You.

And Pedro. Lord, I lift Pedro to You. Father, please protect him of everything evil in that place. May he have the strength to stay away from evil and set himself apart for Your purpose. Lord, I watch him worship, and I wish I could cry upon the name of Jesus again and again, like him. Fresh and new. Lord, be with him. Let your presence comfort him when he feels like he has no comforter. Let your words be his rock. No others. Only Yours. Lord, I don't know why he is there or how long he has to stay, but I pray You use this time to restore him.

Antonio, too. Father, he is so sweet, like a child. I don't know if he ever had a father. Lord, I pray You would give Marco the words to speak so that Antonio can learn Your ways and hold onto them. I pray he would be more eager to learn Your Word than anything else. And protect him, too. Lord, I pray You would just protect him.

Father, so many need You. Lord, send someone their way…

My prayers are but whispers said into my hands, while all here pray aloud, some shouting, others wailing. I continue until I hear others moving about and a voice speaking to the crowd.

Everybody begins to form a large circle in the middle of the room, holding hands. I shyly approach the crowd and two motherly women make room for me and give me their hands. Ministries are announced, and then prayed over, one after another. The types of ministries, I don't know, but the prayers I can understand. Prayers for provision, protection and praises for the same. Then I see Marco step forward and nod in my direction for me to step forward with him. He speaks to the prayer warriors, and I guess by their smiles that this is my official introduction. Judging by the warmth I feel, this is going to be something far more powerful than I could imagine. A few gather around us and begin praying. I feel God's presence in this place, a sweet peace and calm, a comfort and confidence.

The darkness of the night lifts as morning prayer time comes to a close. People talk on the way out, some stopping for coffee and conversation. Marco says a brief goodbye or two, hanging on to his Bible in one hand, his keys in the other.

By the time we get home, the sun has taken over and brought the day with it. Maria is showering when we arrive. It seems early enough to sneak in a few more hours of sleep before reawakening for the day. My mind, however, is too busy predicting our steps at the prison to enjoy any quality sleep.

It is awkwardly silent here. The box television is on only as needed, never serving as background noise. It's definitely not on this morning. The only sounds are porcelain shower tiles being pounded with an inconsistent stream of water pouring out of the hole in the bathroom wall. I cringe, knowing the harsh cold water couldn't possibly be soothing this early in the morning.

Marco sprawls out on his exposed bed and begins reading. His humming is a sweet sound, bringing a forecast of the day of worship we will encounter in a few hours.

The fine line. Few admit it. Yet, we crave it.

4

a few hours later

THE DAY AT THE PRISON starts with voices gathering in the cement shelter that they call their prayer house and somehow ends with me on the basketball court. The windows surround me, looking like a hundred birdcages with bodies perching from them. Their eyes follow me, as my laughter fills the air. The talent streams from the court. Pedro has the whistle in hand. How did they come up with a whistle in here? Then again, it seems like anybody can bring anything in here, provided it passes the so-called security. The prisoners on this side, near the court, seem to be less fortunate than those on the other side. These windows, which are without glass or any protection from the heat or rain, reveal scarce rooms with simple cement slabs and an occasional change of clothing hanging from a window. Three simple bars on each window separate them from me.

I absorb every ounce of this side of the grounds. Two long, identical cement buildings stand across from each other, each housing hundreds of windows, one row on the bottom and one row on the top. If the smell wasn't so awful and the prison walls not so obvious, the buildings themselves wouldn't be that different from the outside of some old dorms back home. In between the two buildings is a cement slab with two basketball hoops without nets, a large grassy area with a few tables and rolling carts with people selling food, and one sidewalk connecting the doorways of the buildings. There are no real doors to open here, just archways. Men are everywhere. Some sitting in the dirt, others in the shade, too many faces to count, many leaning arms out of their cages, rooting for their friends on the basketball court.

I step out from my few brief moments attempting to play ball with these near professionals to take a break on the sidelines. Pedro is built like a model. Near perfection in his abs and height, he wears a face far from eloquent. He runs alongside the others, whistle in hand. The way they run, they way they sweat. They're perfectly normal. Nothing like I would have imagined. No movie depicts this scene. Then again, this isn't scripted.

The game is intense, a few sly shoves and slick moves, a few harsh words, pauses to catch a breath. Smiling, I take a look around.

One of the windows I had frequented with a glance, emptied. Out came Omar. Green eyes. The first thing that runs through my head is that he looks American and might actually speak English. My second thought is he seems to be walking right toward me. Then I realize you can't not notice me. I am the only non-Mexican woman here.

"Hey." A quick nod of his head lets me know he's of this culture, although the absence of an accent says otherwise.

"Hi. I'm Maggie." I start to stand up, but he sits down before I can.

"I know." His eyes stare at mine.

"You know? Well, I don't know yours." I bounce back.

"Omar. You can call me Omar." He says like some serious businessman.

"Ok, Omar. Well, what brought you here?" I manage to match his serious tone quite nicely.

"You waste no time, huh? Here, at this moment, your laugh. It drifted my way, and I had to answer it. Here, the prison? Murder." Still serious.

"Is that so? My laugh? Well, I'll try to keep it better contained next time." My sarcasm is enough to let Omar show a little smile.

"I told you I was in here for murder, so I guess you better." He jokes, and I let a little smile slip through.

"Murder. Huh. Well, we all have our issues." I shrug my shoulders like it's no big deal.

"They say I killed a guy. I did have blood all over when the police got there. My hands were on him. I was trying to see if I could get him to breathe again. I was shaking him, screaming at him..." He looks down at the dry dirt and draws a line with his finger, never once looking up at me.

"Screaming at who?" I look for his eyes, but he avoids me.

"This guy. I didn't even know his name. I don't know what happened, really. I came by my girlfriend's house, and he was there. I didn't do it. I don't even know what happened. They told me he was stabbed a bunch of times. So I guess that's how he died." And with that, I knew Omar's story. He would tell me the story over and over again during the course of my stay in the months to come, adding details, but I never could quite see the day in my mind.

"How long are you here for?" I ask.

"Twelve years. I'll be twenty when my first year's finished in a few months. But, Maggie, it's different here. It's crap. This guy just left last week after paying off the judge to reduce his sentence. He was as guilty as guilty gets, never once denying anything. He killed two guys then a cop. But here, you can pay off anybody. You just have to know the right people and have enough money. If you're rich enough, you never have to see a day in here.

"This side over here is the north side. The poor side. Most of us don't have visitors, and that's the only way you make it here. Your wife or sister brings you food, clothes, TVs, anything. Then you keep it, trade it or sell it. If you don't have someone bringing you money or stuff to trade, you eat beans and rice every day. That's the only free meal around here."

"But I see little stands where people are selling stuff to you guys." There must be eight or ten in here.

"Babe, they aren't selling things to us. They are us. Those guys live here and run a business because someone brings stuff in for them. It's probably what their family lives off of. See that guy over there with the watermelon and ice?" He looks up and nods at an elderly man with a little cart just a few yards away.

"Yeah. I was dying for a taste earlier when Marco set up Bible study under that tree right beside him. I just thought it was an outsider the prison brought in or something."

"His wife brings fruit in every day that visitors are allowed. No more than what will sell, so he doesn't have to deal with everybody jumping him for it. That's why I have to work in the yards. I don't have anybody. I make about 5 pesos a week, that's less than a dollar. But, stuff's cheap. I can get food with that." Omar continues to spill the details of this side of the wall. I listen intently, learning facts I never could have deduced by mere observation.

"So, enough of our world, what are you doing here?" Omar quickly changes his focus.

"Me? I'm going to help Marco for awhile." My honest answer seems to amuse Omar.

"I see." Omar laughs.

"What is that suppose to mean?" I answer, slightly offended.

"Ok, so I've got this gorgeous American chick, about, what, say twenty? I've got this blondy, and let me tell you, a real blonde never walks these grounds. I've got a gorgeous blonde with a sweet childlike voice, not a harsh bone in her body, curves we never get to see, and you think you're going to do something other than draw every eye? I don't think so." Omar makes me want to slap him to show him just how sweet this girl really is.

"Well, I guess I'll just have to show you otherwise." I say, a bit thrown off by his assessment of me.

"Yeah, babe, you will help. Oh, I don't doubt that, with those pouty lips and blue eyes, you'll help Marco a lot. He'll have more guys coming to listen to him than ever before." Omar seems unaware that he's insulting me.

The game finishes with a final blow of the whistle and the guys filter off the court. Pedro glances in my direction a few times before taking a seat next to Marco on the court and guzzling down some warm water. The others come by to say goodbye, with a handshake I haven't yet learned, a kiss on the cheek if they lean in, or a simple nod of the head. I haven't yet learned all of their names. Pedro, of course. Antonio stands out with his tattooed limbs; Jorge asked most of the questions earlier today during our study; Maelo, the kid; Omar was my fifth name. At least ten others seem to routinely wait for Marco's arrival and follow him throughout the day.

Omar looks at me, "You better get over there. You guys have to go in a minute; it's almost 5:00."

"Well, I'm glad you came out here. Everybody speaks Spanish except Pedro, so I have no clue what's going on unless Marco or Pedro fills me in. Well, I'm not just glad because you speak English. That didn't come out right." I put my hand on his shoulder.

"Anything to look into those blue eyes."

Another annoying statement.

"Yeah, whatever." I'm not amused.

"Well, what exactly did you mean?" He backed off.

"I enjoyed talking to you." His green eyes are staring into mine.

"So it's true that you're coming with Marco now? That's what everyone's saying around here, but I'll believe it when I see it." He begins to walk toward his building.

"Boy, rumors spread quickly around here." I respond. With that, Omar disappears and Pedro comes over.

"Hey, girl. Didn't want to keep playing?" Pedro is dripping from head to toe and hasn't yet put his shirt back on, so I make a conscious effort to look into his eyes.

"You guys are serious out there! I couldn't compete with that." I smile and feel his arm on my back for a brief moment, telling me to start walking.

"Yeah, you probably shouldn't be out there running around in this heat anyway." He uses his shirt to wipe the sweat from his forehead, "So, you met Omar, huh?" I can't tell if that is a good thing or not, so I decide to be indifferent.

"Yeah, someone who speaks English." Pedro follows me through the pathway back toward the entrance. We talk while Marco walks with Jorge in nonstop conversation. There is something about Pedro that makes me forget where I am and who I'm with.

"Someone who speaks English, huh? Is that what I am? You're just busy looking for anybody who you can talk to so you're not bored?" Pedro speaks with enough humor to lighten the accusation.

"Yep, that's it. Pedro, the English-speaker." I'm good at this game.

"Is that so? Well, I'll remember to translate critical points next week but stay a distance if not translating. After all, you're using me for my English." He has a way of letting a smile escape if not careful.

"Ok. Sounds good to me. I'll change that to Pedro, the translator.

Is that better?" I turn to look at his expression, but find him already there, waiting to see mine.

"Perfect. Well, Maggie, so nice of you to come today. I will see you next week at approximately nine a.m." Sarcasm fills his words and he has the nerve to bow.

"Shut up! You're making me look like a snot! Don't bow like that." My hand reaches for the bent arm across his waist.

He looks down at the place where my hand meets the skin on his forearm. His eyes don't move. His body doesn't react. He is completely motionless. Have I done something wrong? He had placed his arm on my back once or twice, although quite protectively. Then it occurs to me that he doesn't greet me cheek to cheek like other guys. And he never looks me up and down like so many. No, he only looks into my eyes and follows the movement of my lips. Nothing more. Nothing inappropriate.

I look up and our eyes meet. My hand moves closer to his hand as I simply say, "Sorry."

Pedro reaches for my hand and squeezes my fingers quickly once, as if to say something. Then he turns away. I watch as he waits a moment to be given a chance to say goodbye to Marco, who kisses him fondly on the forehead. Pedro doesn't look back at me again.

The line.

5

a few weeks later, tuesday morning

After just weeks, the faces here are becoming familiar. More of them know my name than I know theirs. Mostly, they know my route through the paths to the furthest building - Pedro's. They know I go to his cell. They know he walks nearly everywhere with me. Unlike one might think, not a single man touches any portion of me as I walk by. For me, there is never an ounce of fear or hesitation. The presence of God radiates in this place. His protection is the core of my peace here. So when Marco asked if I would be comfortable getting Pedro in the mornings, I never thought of saying no. I have no reason to fear. For me, prayer in the tent church leaves me eager for the day, feeling the presence of God surrounding us, confirming my call to this place, despite the skeptics.

"Pedro. You awake?" I yell as I knock twice on his plywood door, a fair attempt at privacy in this otherwise bar-filled place. His room is in the back half of the cell, separated by another sheet of plywood. After just a few days, it seems like his roommate has grown accustomed to my morning wake up call. I hear Spanish somethings floating about, and decide to sit on the slight step that separates the wall of cells from the walkway, just outside his door.

The overweight stomachs here are as unappealing as my dad's back home. Four or five guys sit across from me sporting flab and jeans. The morning air is affected the moment we drive into the prison parking lot, but it's almost unbearable right here. Despite the unbreatheable stench, at least the air isn't yet baking with heat.

The sounds of a shower in a nearby cell are the only sounds this morning. Guys seem to be waiting for something to draw them out of their cells, to get their morning started, to bring some purpose to their day. Most guys are sitting in their cells staring at me, as though I am that something. For some, I am. For Pedro, my knock means a morning devotion and morning worship. For me, the time here *is* what is happening.

"Hey Maggie. How are ya?" Pedro walks out with his Bible in hand, ready for the day.

"Good. It's nice out this morning. Did you have a good night last night?" I stand up to walk with him, finding myself drawn to the cologne that comes with the freshly showered Pedro.

"Yeah. We played cards, sat around. Nothing much. What about you?" He nods at his neighbors as we make our way outside the building and into the yards.

"I didn't do much either. Rosie and I talked until she went out with friends. Then I just sat around thinking until I fell asleep." Thinking about everything I'm sure this man would never imagine would run through this girl's head. Him, them, being here, not one thought about anything else.

We make our way to the chain link pathways and Pedro takes the first step in, I follow him, as close as possible, letting him be the buffer to the men that continuously approach me.

I've learned quickly that I can't walk in the closed pathways alone without stopping and being surrounded by a group of men, some offering me knick-knacks, others asking me things in Spanish that I just can't understand. The men are polite, quiet, not to mention almost always "innocent" in their own eyes. They walk before me, beside me, lounging about the crowded paths. Simple eyes often meet mine and stumble over English, pushing out a "Please?" Pedro patiently waits as new faces gaze toward mine. I meet them with brief "hellos" and kisses upon the cheek. He eases a sweet smile their direction as another borrows me for a moment. I never know if it will be a request for a drink from my oversized water bottle or an offer for a recently carved cedar figurine. But most often, it is a pleading pair of eyes needing mine. I don't know if it's the rarity of a woman in a world filled with men, or a shade of blue in the midst of so many browns, but I know that my eyes were created for these very moments. I listen to them connect my eyes to their tales of an old flame, a missed mother, of a time far from here.

After taking over ten minutes to make our way about fifty feet, we finally arrive for worship. Pedro sweetly allows me to pass through first then follows after.

"Buenos días, Pedro. Cómo estás, mijo?" Marco greets Pedro with a hug. He has gathered a few guys so far: Maelo, Antonio, Jorge, who fooled me into thinking he was a visitor my first day in his professional-looking polo, and a guy who came for the first time yesterday.

Marco and Pedro start talking, so I give them space and take a minute to say hello to the guys. Maelo comes right over and greets me with a kiss on the cheek. I still can't imagine this shy baby-faced child doing something horrific enough to end up in here. Marco would've told me if it was something minor. I can't imagine. I just can't imagine. He's just sixteen, barely grown. I have only seen Maelo in a white tank top and black gym shorts, so I'm guessing he lives on the poor side and spends his time watching other people have visitors.

Maelo nods at me, the common conversation starter here. I nod back. We're stuck in a language gap. My Spanish is improving, but I have no real references, books, or other methods of studying. I only have constant exposure, and that's even compromised because Marco's perfectly bilingual family caters to me.

"Qué onda?" I use the phrase I hear Rosie and Victor use all the time with their friends at the house. A simple, "What's up?"

His fast Spanish leaves me saying, "más despacio por favor" over and over as we attempt to get to know each other. I don't think we cover more than the fact that we're both doing ok, but I can see into his naked eyes. The kind of eyes that look everywhere but straight into yours. The kind of eyes that tell the real story, while the mouth moves to tunes of another. The eyes that still miss Mamá, long for a lap to sink back into, and cradle the grown child to bed on a cement slab. Those kind of eyes. I like him. I see something there that is too childlike to have committed anything without years of sculpting. Somehow, this once babe in diapers wasn't given the tools to stay on the other side. His eyes bleed. The way yours and mine never will.

In my limited Spanish, I ask, "Cuánto tiempo más, Maelo?" I know my Spanish is bad, but he somehow manages to understand that I want to know how much more time he has in here.

"No sé." Maelo tells me he doesn't know. He doesn't know how much more time?

"Está bien." I give up, but Maelo walks to Marco. He waits for him to notice and waves for me to come over.

"Maelo wants to know what you asked him," Marco explains.

"I just asked him how long he'll be here." I say, looking at Maelo, expecting a number, but instead I sit and listen to several exchanges between the two. Minutes later, Marco fills me in, Maelo's eyes clearly looking for my reaction.

"Well, Maggie, it's one of those unpleasant things about Mexico that's so different from the United States." Marco looks at me, "Maelo hasn't gone to court yet." His hand reaches for my arm, predicting my immediate reaction.

"What? You have to be kidding me! You told me he got here last year. You said he's been here for a year! What do you mean he hasn't been to court?" I'm as upset as Marco expects me to be.

"Let me explain." Marco pauses for too long and gets me even more irritated.

"Maelo was accused of doing something, and there were people who turned in his name. He was arrested, and the court date was set for a year down the road. They bring the arrested here to wait for their court dates. For Maelo, it was suppose to be this month, but he got a notice last week that it's been pushed back to October."

"He hasn't been found guilty?" I am shocked. This is so beyond my understanding that I can't even ask intelligent questions.

"No, he hasn't. He hasn't gone in front of the judge. He was accused. So far, he was just accused. Now, in the States, you put them in jail to post bail. Here, they go to prison and wait," Marco explains.

"Marco, he's a kid. He's in here with murderers and rapists and who knows what. What is this teaching him? What if he's innocent? So he just loses his life in the meantime?"

"Yes, and if he's found innocent, he walks out."

"Ok, so why is it taking so long to hear his case?" I ask.

"Maggie. Maelo will be convicted." Marco looks at me then looks at Maelo, knowing he can't understand. I feel like we're discussing a secret in front of the person that told us not to tell.

"I'm not following you. Do you know what happened? Why do

you think that? Did he confess?" My eyes squint as the questions fume from my lips.

"He's a street kid, Maggie. His family doesn't have any money. They can't pay for a lawyer. They can't pay for his court date to be pushed up. They can't pay the judge to rule in his favor." His words kill me. It's this kind of injustice that tears at my soul.

I can tell my quest for justice is one Marco has battled as well. He simply tells me that we're not here to change the corruption. We're here to change lives.

Marco's gentle hand squeezes mine tightly before reaching for his guitar.

"Let's head to the north side and set up worship over there this morning. I think we can get some more guys to join us." With that, we pack up and head out to find some shade.

Omar comes skipping toward me and greets me with a quick kiss on the cheek.

"Hey gorgeous," he smiles.

"Hey. Where ya off to?" I ask, sensing some hurrying.

"I gotta go see somebody; I'll be back in awhile." He grabs my hand briefly.

Pedro walks over to Omar and greets him with the handshake they all use. Pedro's eyes watch Omar grab my hand again and give it a squeeze before taking off. "I'll see you in awhile, ok?" He kisses my cheek again and hurries off.

"He likes you, Maggie." Pedro says while watching Omar head toward the south side.

"Why shouldn't he?" I naively ask, truly unaware of what Pedro is thinking.

"Sweetheart, he really likes you. You need to make sure he isn't thinking you are hanging out with him because there's interest, ya know?" Pedro's words are ridiculous. Omar and I are friends.

"Pedro, we spend an hour or more talking everyday. Omar is like a brother to me. He is not *into* me. Believe me, I know. And he just listens to me. He wants to know about everything I've seen and done to get his mind off things here. He's not into me, really." I believe every word.

"His face lights up when he sees you." Pedro insists.

"What do you want me to do? Everybody is happy to see me. I mean, everybody's desperate for attention in here." I say, getting a little irritated with his persistence and then feeling bad that I've just implied he's desperate for attention, too.

"Just be aware. Omar's a great guy, really. And I'd tell you if it was a problem. Just let your conversation with him focus on what we've discussed in Bible study, so you know he's getting what's important." Pedro's right, and I'm thankful that he cares about Omar. Pedro seems older the more time I spent with him, more mature than many of the others, definitely more grounded in the Word.

"I know. We've read all of Ephesians twice this week while Marco has been studying it with you guys. I pray with him, and he says he prays every night. I believe him. I don't know if he ever prayed until he heard Marco leading. He is growing." I say.

Marco overhears our conversation, "Good. Glad to here it. Now *you*, you come here." He pulls me close and hugs me, kissing the top of my head. Marco looks over at Pedro and smiles, "She's ok. I'm watching her." Pedro looks into my eyes without an expression on his face, although something is happening in that head of his.

One side of the building is shaded in the mornings, so we sit there to start off the day. Marco strums the guitar and belts out worship music in a voice loud enough to wake any sleeping somebody. That's the cue for our guys to emerge from their cells. Maelo sings quietly;

Pedro sings loudly, sitting right next to me. Jorge looks over notes he brought with him, maybe lyrics, maybe Bible notes, who knows. The man with the watermelon greets his wife just a few feet away. She hums along with Marco' tunes.

Although the words are foreign and the melody surpassed, the music speaks to me. The music itself refuels my soul with a sweetness that comes from closing in with God. My eyes close as the men's voices increase in number and volume. I never once look up to see who has joined us, I simply sit, knees and chin meeting at my chest, absorbing the vocal offerings of these precious men.

One voice scratchy, another in tune, one deep, another high and loud. Others confident, some barely whispering along. The difference between this choir and one of trained musicians is truly astounding. These men sing with the realization that their sin no longer paves their paths, affects their beings, dominates their decisions. These men sing with joy to the Savior of their souls. The sound of joy among so much sorrow rises up. My eyes freely cry, as I struggle to hide the deep breaths that push my back in and out.

Lord, thank You. Thank You for letting me be here, in this place, to hear this worship right now. Lord, forgive me for not worshipping You for all You've done, for not feeling the significance of Your sacrifice. Lord… I am amazed that these men have found You in this place of bitterness. They all hurt, Lord. They all hurt. Oh Lord, bring to us those that need You most and don't know where, who, or what to turn to. Father, soften their hearts. Let this music sink into their spirits. Bring them to us, Lord, so we can share Your Word with them. I just pray that Marco be especially sensitive to You today. That he will know what to say to the guys who need comfort and peace. And Father, I pray that You meet them and fill them with Your peace that surpasses all understanding. That's what we all need, Lord. That peace that we can't get on our own. Jesus, thank You for all You're doing in these lives. I pray You touch each one here as we minister to them today. Help their eyes be opened even wider than ever before, so Your ways can transform them.

My eyes lift to find Marco smiling with his chin up in the air, his body swaying to the beat of a slower song. Wearing the blue wife beater he wears every day, Antonio sings his heart out. A man in a button down collared shirt has also joined us. There are seven this morning. Pedro's eyes are closed, Bible in hand, a tear on his cheek, another quickly following. The music quietly drifts, and Marco opens with an all-Spanish prayer.

Ephesians is coming to a close. A few hours of study for several days was ample time, and Marco says there are so many important books of the Bible that we need to move on. Today is the last day for questions. The man in the collared shirt immediately starts asking questions, which is strange since he has never attended before. The questions are a little over a new believer's head, so Marco takes him and Jorge aside and asks Pedro to answer questions for anybody else. I stay to help Pedro.

Antonio is our first, second, and only question. Pedro is so gentle and patient, taking time to explain each verse and how they come together to say something about Antonio's life right now. Pedro's shirt is tucked in to a black belt; his hair gelled back, his shoes barely worn. His eyes are their eyes. They all desire something good and true and worthy of their time. They're finding it here. Just a little late. Too late to keep them from this place, yet early enough to live a transformed life.

My eyes watch Pedro explain a specific prayer in the first chapter to the rest of the guys. He glances toward me, and gives me a sweet smile, as if to say, "Are you hanging in there? I know you don't understand." But I do. My English Bible is open to the same page, and I can amazingly grasp nearly all Spanish when we have Bible study.

Marco told me that he used to meet with Pedro for an hour by himself each morning. That was it. No time in worship. No group studies. He said over the past two years, Pedro has grown immensely, becoming the one that Marco depends on more than any other.

I can see it in the way that Pedro encourages others not just with words but also with touch. I can't imagine the ache for affection, the longing for any sort of physical touch. I never see any of these guys hugging each other like on the outside. In this place, the cultural norm is lost. Handshakes prevail. Marco does all the hugging, patting backs, and kissing foreheads. Pedro nearly always grabs an arm, gives a friendly pat on the back or a firm grab of a shoulder when he meets these guys each morning, affections rarely accepted here. Such subtleties pop in a place like this; there is no need to study the behaviors; they are quite obvious. Every inch of the grounds are the same; all interactions very similar: feeling out one another, staring down, passing things from hand to hand, rare smiles from man to man, distance between all bodies.

As Pedro's fingers move from left to right along the words in his Bible, each man diligently leans toward him for prayer. Pedro begins praying the words we talked about on my first day over each man. Ephesians 1:19. He reads the words aloud, the name of each man added in to personalize the scripture, "I also pray that Antonio will understand the incredible greatness of God's power for us who believe him." Though not in the group with them, I can feel the warmth exuding from this small circle of men. The circle marks an intimacy of a new sort, true and long sought-after family within the walls.

"Maggie," Marco's voice interrupts my stares, "I need to talk with Jorge a little more. You can relax. It's hot. You brought money? Go buy an ice drink, dear. Today's good for that. You have lots of time. It's only 11:00." Marco is thirsty for teaching today. We typically only touch the surface.

"Ok." I sit up, brush the dry dirt off the back of my pants, and grab my water bottle.

"I'll come with you." Pedro says. He gets up and joins me.

"How are you this morning? Are you catching anything?" He squints to fight through the sun.

"I'm good. Glad to be here. Yeah, God's been opening up my understanding when I step into this place. It's amazing. I can really understand what you're saying and your explanations. But I leave here in the afternoon and can barely buy a Coke down the street without fumbling over my words. It clicks on and off. Literally." I smile and reach for the change in my pocket.

"God's like that. He gives you what you need at the moment. That's one lesson I've definitely learned in here." I follow his eyes as he glances toward the armor stationed on the wall extending the perimeter of the prison. The off-white paint is as well-weathered as the armor seems to be. They sit on corners with large guns, holding them as if waiting for a chance to use them. They look at the grounds and see something I could never see. And that's why they live on the mounted wall. It's why they are posed in armor. Their uniformed bodies stare down and see worthless beings. Nothing more.

I glance about at the endless rows of barred windows and see faces looking out at me, at the sky, probably up at the armor as well. Most windows are hugged by muscular arms with noticeable ribs. Men everywhere. Stuck here.

Armor here and there. Here on their own accord. What makes a man want to stand on these prison walls? What exactly motivates a man to see another man in such a way?

The fine line creeps up within me. The line that draws them here. The line that justifies their harsh stares. The line that encourages armor, guns, and the use of them. The line that separates those down here from those up there.

I finally take a minute to ask Pedro what I've been wanting to know since my first day, "How much longer do you have?" The first thing I want to know about everyone.

"How much longer? Well, I'm doing eight years. I've done thirty-one months. It's depressing, huh? I can barely handle it some days. There's only so much cologne to hide the smell. You would think I would have gotten used to it after all this time, but sometimes I can barely breathe. It has to affect you. It's waste. And then there are the nights. They're the worst. I just want to fall asleep the minute it gets dark. There are only so many forms of entertainment. You wouldn't believe what games you can invent when you're bored." Pedro pauses while I hold up three fingers, requesting three iced watermelon drinks for a peso each.

"I don't know why you come, Maggie. I see you every morning." His defined cheekbones can't contain a smile. "Well, I hear you at my door every morning and I'm surprised. I know you say you're coming, but I don't expect you to. It's easier not to expect it because at some point, you won't knock. Then I won't…" He stops.

"You won't *what?*" I have no idea where he is going with this, but his seriousness surprises me.

"I won't go to sleep knowing you'll be there when I wake up." Pedro turns from me the moment the words come out. I want to hug him close, to let him feel an actual hug from a woman. I want him to know that I live and breathe this place. That my mind doesn't turn off and rejoice the moment I step back into my world. In fact, it does quite the opposite. I find myself wondering what their side is doing. I long to know this world around the clock, instead of just in the light of the day.

"I know I have something to do, someone is waiting for me to get up and do something with myself during the day. It's so easy to not do anything. Your soft voice makes me want to be better. I want to open that door and see you. I want to know the joy that carries you here. You amaze me." Pedro's words are slowly being stored in my long-term memory.

"Some small town girl amazes you?" I don't know what to say, so I try to insert some humor.

"I don't see anyone else coming here every day to hang out with scum like us."

I interrupt him, "Don't say that. I'm serious, Pedro. That's crap. You're just people." The watermelon man nods and places three perfect slushes in front of me.

"I know. But that's what we are to them." His throat gulps out loud as he looks away. "But that's not my point. My point is you are here, spending your time doing whatever you can for us." He speaks sincerely.

"It's funny you say that 'cuz I feel like I'm doing next to nothing. I can't speak to anyone but you and Omar. I feel useless." It's the truth.

"You don't have to say a word. Don't you see, Maggie? These men that see you here everyday are seeing the love of Christ. They see some young American girl coming here when she could be anywhere. That makes them wonder. They want to know what draws you here. They know it's not me or Antonio, or even Marco. They're smarter than that. So if you never sing another song or speak to anyone, God is still using you to show them that He cares. He ministers to everybody everywhere. He shines right through that gorgeous smile." His hand briefly touches my cheek as his words answer the very questions that live within me.

The fine line, a dividing wall to everyone else, a thin thread, transparent to me.

6

friday afternoon

DAYS COME TO AN END. Depressing sometimes, relieving once in awhile. But mostly, it's the same. The metal of the door handle to the Bronco inevitably burns my fingers and the seat scorches through my jeans. The rim of Marco's sombrero gives him a bit of shade while we battle the graveled holes in the path they call a street. The streets lead us to the worst homes imaginable, sheets on poles protecting bare children from the sun. The bumps lift me from my seat, and I stare out the window. Sometimes Marco tells of a great talk with a new man who will now see heaven. Those are the days when it's all worth it. I smile, impressed at the way God works, and at the way I've come to love it here. I lose my seat in between dozes and tiptoe with bracing myself on the feverish mantle of the car. My heart always fights with leaving. I want to crawl beneath the rules and stay just one night to know the silence, the silence that lives where freedom does not. I think Marco would tell me it's the same silence that he hears me going through at night. That same silence we all experience from time to time. The silence that haunts you when your soul longs to be somewhere else. I wipe the sweat from my hairline and lean out the window, hoping to feel a breeze until we make it home.

Victor is lounging across the couch; a fan, failing to reel in a breeze, blocks the front door. Diego scrunches his nose to bump his glasses up into place and Marco steps over the fan and heads straight for the shower. Maria kisses my cheek and wipes her soapy hands on her skirt, offering me her hand to step over the fan. The sounds of Diego's high-pitched cartoons are the only sounds this afternoon. Maria tells me about two girls from the States coming to stay a week while working in an orphanage. I can't help wondering how two more will fit in our two-bedroom home. The sound of water pounding on cement stops.

Freshly showered, Marco sits down to relax a bit before ironing his shirt. I don't know if my lack of listening skills interfered, or if I was just distracted, but before long he, Maria, and Diego are gone. Only Victor and I are left. They have Friday night service at the tent church, and I didn't realize they were already leaving. So, here I sit. Another night.

"Hey, what's up with you?" Victor is social tonight. A rarity.

"Not much. Just another normal day." I'm tired and still have a lot on my mind, so I'm not overly social.

"No, really. What'd you guys do today? Did you talk to anyone?" I guess Victor does have some interest.

"Pedro mostly." I sit on the loveseat across from him, our legs only a few feet apart.

"Ah, Pedro. Yeah, he's cool actually." Victor seems sincere.

"You know Pedro?" I'm suddenly interested in conversing.

"I've just gone with my dad a couple times when he's made me. We always stop by Pedro's, bringing him books, talking to him forever. So I've chatted with him a few times. He's a nice guy. Dumb to get caught, but nice." Victor has a way of saying exactly what he means all the time.

"Well that was mean." I'm not surprised at his comment, but it bothers me.

"Oh, geez, Maggie. So sensitive. I was joking, dear." He throws the couch pillow at me.

"Don't call me 'dear'." I snottily reply.

"Oh, you love it." Victor flirts in the way that always brings the other American girls into flirtation mode. But it has never worked on me.

"Pedro's different. I know he's there, but I just kinda like him." I freely say.

"You actually like him? Maggie, he's not even attractive." Victor sits up, suddenly interested himself.

"He is too! He's attractive in every way that you're not." I'm harsh, on purpose.

"Is that so? Hey, I'm not saying I'm gorgeous or anything, but I never considered Pedro handsome. Don't get me wrong, he's a nice guy, really. I can joke around with him and everything. I just don't see how you'd find anybody in there attractive. Are you feeling ok? Need some Tylenol or something heavier?" Victor sarcastically asks.

"Funny. No, I'm fine. What do you care who I like anyway?" I'm anxious for a response from the guy who is out with friends so often he hasn't taken any time to get to know me.

"I care. I mean I don't care, care. But I don't want to see you actually fall for a guy in there. My dad would freak out, and you're all emotional anyways, without a reason. I can't imagine the drama if you actually had a reason for it." He smiles with satisfaction.

"Victor, I can't stand you." I mean every word.

This is the first time we've had to put up with each other for more than a week on a mission trip. This living under the same roof is a whole new challenge.

"Oh, Maggie. Calm down, I love ya. You know it." I get up and go to Rosie's bedroom. I fall on her bed and sleep the evening away.

I wake up to the sounds of Marco tuning his guitar and bits of oil popping on the stovetop. Maria is making popcorn, the frequent dinner replacement. I reach for drops for my contacts and glance at the clock: 8:00. That early? A whole night still to come.

"Hola, Maggie. How are ju, dear?" Maria's warm voice trickles in, as she wipes her hands on her floor-length skirt and sits down beside me.

"Tired." Her arm reaches around me, and my head rests on her shoulder. Her freshly dyed black hair is pulled back tightly. She smells like a mom, a light flowery scent coming off of her arms.

"Are you hungry?" She asks.

"No. I'm just kind of blah. I want to read a little. I'm sorry I missed church." I really am sorry.

"We decided to escape before ju could come. Ju need rest, dear. The heat in the summer is too hot for ju body. I told Marco to keep ju drinking all day. So, dear, ju rest tonight, so ju can do the Lord's work tomorrow." Everything Maria says is true. I need rest.

Our fourth worship earlier in the day had started a little after 3:00 in Antonio's cell. It was so hot today that the grounds looked vacant; everyone took a break from the heat. We did one outside worship time early, but even inside wasn't refreshing. The day was overwhelming. The cell was completely empty. Nothing but two "bunks," which were actually molds of cement sticking out from the wall. Another cement wall provided a divider from the hole that served as a toilet and the other hole, which served as a shower. There were no towels, toilet paper, shoes, or a change of anything. There was simply a sheet folded on his roommate's top bunk. There was nothing to straighten or clean. Sitting in that cell today was the first time I truly felt the prison, as I imagined a prison to be.

About fifteen men formed a circle and sang along with Marco. The prayer time was when I lost it. It was so hot, and we were standing for so long. Prayer must have been over an hour because each man was being called into the circle for prayer. I finally began to sway. Pedro held me up with an arm on my elbow then walked me to Antonio's bunk. Someone rushed out and brought back some cold water. I hadn't been drinking nearly enough water because the water in my bottle was so hot and just didn't ease my thirst. The cold water Pedro handed me was refreshing. My first water with ice in weeks.

Marco started praying over me, and the men joined in. I don't know what they said. I just remember Marco rubbing cold ice over my forehead. I woke up to Pedro holding a white, cool cloth on my head, the others gone except Marco, who was packing up his guitar. So went my first encounter with dehydration and fatigue. It had only taken three weeks to happen.

Maria leaves my room and closes the door on her way out. I take out my Bible and begin reading in Acts, our next study. My eyes see the words, but all my mind sees are the men.

I want to be seen with them. I want to be seen with him. I want the world to see me with him so they can understand. And with all the tears, with all the words said, this is only for me. Marco says few can actually come to the prison and get it. And I am one.

I never get to go home and tell about it. I think of my mother and imagine her going off on one of her tangents. My insecurities, my never-ending quest for the impossible. She could never handle my days here. She'd probably go along with the people who say Pedro's too pathetic to deserve any more than he has. I hope they spend hours struggling to understand how the only punishment he faces is that within him – hitting him no matter what side of the wall.

I find myself growing angry and frustrated until I slowly slip into a deep sleep.

A sleep with no lines at all.

7

early tuesday morning

4:30 A.M. ROLLS AROUND TOO soon. The ever-welcome cool breeze still leaps in the window, and the night sky looks darker than the one the morning before. Marco's whisper in the room is a one-time only wake up call, so I quickly grab for any available pants and change my shirt into something with sleeves. The front screen door shuts with an abnormally loud bang of metal meeting doorframe, and I quickly wet my face and exchange glasses for contacts, as Marco starts up the engine.

The bumps of the city streets and the quick swerving of the car to avoid them are enough to keep me awake on the fifteen-minute trip to the tent church. Every day, the same route. Every day, completely lost for direction. Sometimes, for the sake of mental stimulation, I attempt to find a landmark and locate it the next day, but I never do. So I conclude that Marco has multiple never-to-be-repeated routes to the tent church, or I simply have no business ever driving anywhere in Mexico.

The usual amount gather for prayer, fifty, maybe even seventy-five. We scatter on the slab and spend our hour engaging in conversation with Jesus. Hearts are breaking as voices burst through the silences. Souls are aching as bodies tremble and women beg through tears.

The cries erase the language barrier and reveal the souls within. Some stand strong and firm, pacing in straight paths, others fall before the Lord, voices lifting despite being level with the ground. My eyes glance about, watching so many filled with joy, sorrow, pain. My curiosity overshadows my needs, drifting me far from prayer and into a world of wonder.

How did I end up here? How could I ever go back home? Is Pedro awake? Antonio? Would Omar come today? Any of our guys? Did they sleep in the deepest darkness, or did they too awaken to metal bars meeting doorframes? Could they smell sweetbread cooking, like the one drifting my direction now? Who was I kidding… sweetbread. Did they ache at all hours, or especially these… the time in the night when silence breeds loneliness. *Or do they call upon you, Lord? Do they lift Your name and do the very things Marco teaches in the day? Do they wait upon You and trust You completely? Do they pray or drift, like me?*

Oh Father, Precious Lord, teach me to cope. To deal. To dwell on Your goodness and plan, not on their daily struggles. Give me Your understanding, along with compassion. Teach me, Lord, because I can't see justice. I only see Your mercy. I can't see your forgiveness and their punishment side by side. Are you pleased with this, Lord?

Do you want these men in there? New believers? How will their faith survive? How will they have others to show them how to follow You? I pray You send Your angels to watch over them until their time is done. Lord, show me Your ways. I have no understanding. No understanding. Help me, Lord.

"Vamos a orar por todos Los Ministerios de la Iglesia, vengan ustedes." I stretch my legs before getting up to join Marco in the circle, relieved that I spent at least a few moments spilling to the Lord.

Prayer. Group prayer.

The ride home is as bumpy as the one there. Although Marco's mouth is moving and words are coming out, I find myself drifting once again.

Marco is filled with the joy that allows him to cross the fine line every day. The same joy that led me to the Lord and has guided me so many times. The joy I now feel conditionally. Joy that bursts when I see them worship the Lord, ask questions, and begin to wrap their minds around new concepts, when I see them come find us in the mornings, wanting more of Christ.

My world has suddenly collided with theirs. A collision of bizarre sorts. A collision that causes my joy to dissipate when I leave and awaken when I arrive. A collision inside the world of being locked up, confined, monitored by gun-wearing guards, forced to stay. A collision that takes me to the soul of the man, the heart of the hurt, the reality of regret.

The Bronco pulls up to our little cement home. Maria meets us with a kiss on the cheek and a slightly burned piece of peanut butter toast on the dining table for me and an egg for Marco. As I stop and remind myself that she sweetly remembered my love for peanut butter and had to make toast on a cast iron skillet, I smile and actually enjoy the crunch. As Marco reaches over and pushes play, I hurriedly jump up and claim the shower before music wakes the entire house.

The freezing water never fails to shock me in the mornings. I jump in it for a split second to get wet then dodge it until I have to rinse. The worship music flows into the shower with me, bringing all my frustrations out once again. I let the stream of water hit the tile to create privacy in this crammed shared space, and I finally cry freely.

Pounding water frees my fears, and I cry out to God. *Lord, thank You for this time, for these moments, for each day that I've been able to go to the prison. But Lord, why Lord? Why do I have such a need to be there? Why don't I turn it all off at night? Why can't I just put it aside? They're just people, Lord.*

Just people. God, help me turn this all off. Help me walk out of there. They need so much. And Maelo, he's just a boy! Lord, how will this precious child survive in there… how will he survive? Do You care? Do You care about them? What am I thinking even asking You this? I know You care. Oh, I know You care. I'm so lost in all of this. I'm so tired of caring, of thinking of them all the time. Will they ever be loved, Lord? Ever? Take this burden from me, please.

A harsh knock on the door stops my crying. I wipe yesterday's mascara from my eyes with the thin towel and dry off in a hurry. Still damp, I slip my foot into the only washed jeans I have and quickly dress. Devotions are about to begin. I fake it well, smiling has always come easy for me, so this will be a breeze. Or so I thought.

An hour later, the Bronco passes another shoeless child roaming about in the morning, and Marco simply asks, "Maggie, why were you crying this morning?"

"Could you hear me? I'm so sorry! I tried…" His words interrupt mine, "No, dear, I couldn't hear you. I could see your sadness. Your smile doesn't fool me." I had suspected it for a long time, but it was in that moment that I knew both Marco and I truly see the soul.

"I just don't think it's fair." My vague answer covers the many thoughts causing my tears. So much isn't fair.

"Hmm. Not fair. We can talk about fairness. Do you want to talk about fairness, or do you want to talk about something that really matters?" He must be kidding. To think that fairness doesn't matter. Has he lost his mind? Fairness. Really?

"What really matters, Marco?" I can barely spit out the question, knowing I don't want to hear his answer.

"Oh, Maggie, so much, my Love. So much. It's the soul; it's not justice on this earth. The soul is alive no matter where the body is. They may not have the opportunities we have, and some lost those opportunities for good reasons, others maybe not. Those aren't the things that should be on your mind."

Words I could've spit out to someone else, I'm sure, but either way, they don't take away the ache within. With each day that goes by, I grow closer to them. Hours watching them interact, days of conversations with Omar and Pedro, time with all the others. My nine to five is addictive. The weekends away drive me crazy, well, our weekends. Saturday is a visitation day at the prison, so we are there. Sunday and Monday, however, are off-limits. My longest days. With so much time walking the grounds, aren't these feelings normal? Is something wrong with me?

"Marco?" My voice is breaking. I nearly bump my head on the visor as Marco quickly swerves to miss a pothole. We're almost there.

"Yes, Maggie." Marco patiently answers.

"I'm sorry," I quietly manage to say, "I just love them." Simple but true.

Smiling, he grabs my hand and holds on to it until we pull up to the parking lot.

We approach the first door, give over our IDs, and find ourselves face-to-face with two guards. The only ones in this place that I can count on to look me up and down without hesitation or subtlety.

So begins my worst day yet.

Some wait for us on the other side of the thickest black door each morning but rarely Pedro. I look forward to going to his building and knocking on the plywood façade.

I can almost predict the men and position I'll find each in as I walk to get Pedro: burgundy jeans leaning on the first wall, old man singing to me from the fenced-in infirmary walking with me along the fence until I pass, sleeping men slumped over in my pathway, forcing me to move to the side, lift a foot, make it around them, then an open dirt yard, absent of all men. Inside his building, it is always the same: a cart on the right with chick-lets and Mexican candy, run by an older man who never buttons his shirt, most cell doors closed, and a few voices here and there. Nine o'clock is still an early wake up call for most here. I walk to the line of cells in front of me and knock on the second door.

This morning, Pedro's roommate peeks through an opening, calls for him, and opens the door toward me, motioning for me to come in. My first invitation. Hearing Pedro's voice puts me at ease and I step in. To my left is an actual counter filled with pans and cans of beans on the bottom, clean on the top, and to my right is a bed. Perfectly made. In front of me is another piece of plywood covering the rest of the room, nearly the entire width. I can see the cut out of a door and hinges screwed in. His roommate opens the door back up and nods at me as he leaves. Just a foot from the bed and an arm's length from the counter, I stand in the middle of the room until Pedro's voice calls from behind a curtain hanging near the counter.

"Maggie, have a seat. I'm just getting out of the shower. Give me just a minute."

"Ok." I need a minute to visually absorb this place he calls home. A clean tiled floor, a place for every pot, every pan, two plates and several forks, a little black burner with its cord wrapped nicely underneath, two lemons, sheets under the blanket, a pillow and even a mini dorm fridge. Pedro's place is much more livable than Antonio's.

"Hey," Pedro steps into the room wearing only dark jeans and an unfastened black belt. He towel dries his long black hair, drips finding his bare chest. In the ten seconds it takes him to move from there to the plywood door near me, I don't think I blink. This man is gorgeous.

"Sorry if I'm too early," I am so distracted that I'm just thankful I can get the words out.

"No, not at all." As Pedro turns toward me, I can't help but notice horrible bruising along his right ribs. "My alarm didn't go off this morning, so I woke up figuring you'd be here any second," he realizes my eyes aren't meeting his, and he follows them to his chest.

"Pedro, what happened?" I have never seen bruising that covered such a large area.

"I'll be fine." With that, he opens the little plywood door and disappears into the other room. I look around, feeling awful for asking.

"Pedro?" I hope he knows I'm not going to push the issue anymore.

"Just a sec, Maggie. I've just got to grab my Bible." He comes out in a black fitted V-neck already tucked in, Bible in hand.

"Hey, I didn't mean to ask… I just…" I feel so dumb.

"Maggie, I left my shirt on my bed. I had no idea you'd be here so quick, and I didn't realize he'd let you in. I didn't want you to see." Honesty is easy to detect, and this man is honest.

"I'm sorry. I should've waited outside. He just opened the door, and I guess I was wondering what your place looked like." Hoping he could see my sincerity, I stand up to leave.

"No, that's not what I'm saying. You are… Uh. Maggie, having you here is… You know what, come see the place." His long hair meets his jawline, hiding his full smile, but it is there.

"Well, show me around!" Without a thought, I grab his left arm and duck down to follow him through the plywood door to the other half of the room. In addition to the cement slab beds is another complete bed taking up the majority of the space.

"This is my bed. That's his." He points to the slab that is hidden beneath a mattress and plenty of blankets. The top bunk isn't a bunk at all. It has perfectly folded clothes in stacks, a closet of sorts. Across from that, Pedro's bed seems to be handmade just for this place, complete with drawers that pull out underneath. On his headboard is a bottle of cologne and a bookmark next to a pen and small notebook. A pair of shoes is on the floor, placed neatly beside the bed. A large fan going full blast sits inside the barred window. Cool air blows in along with a horrid smell. Pedro guesses what I'm thinking and squirts his cologne in front of the fan.

"What are you thinking, Maggie? You sorry you came?" Embarrassment catered his every word. He stands by the fan, looking out the window, as far from me as possible in this six by eight space.

"No." I am really not. "I was actually wondering how you managed to get that bed in here." Raising my eyebrows, I wait for some fancy explanation.

His sweet smile comes back, "Well, I have family close by. My parents came by a few times my first year, and showed up with it one day. My papa built it for me."

"So, people can bring anything in here?" He sits down on his bed and pats the space next to him. I sit down, too close to him.

"I wouldn't say anything, but yes, lots of things. Everything in here came from my parents. My roommate is from Mexico City, so we take care of him, too. He doesn't get visitors." He looks up at the ceiling as he answers me.

"So, Antonio, I guess he's alone here, too?" I couldn't bear to think of spending my nights on a cement slab, no cushion, no pillow, nothing humane about it.

"Yeah." His eyes meet mine.

"Yeah." I bite my upper lip, absorbing this new world.

"It's amazing how quickly it becomes home. Really. Well, it's not home like yours or the one I had back home, but it's where I live now, and it's just the way it is." Pedro speaks with maturity, not even a hint of emotion or frustration within him.

This whole idea of home hits me hard. My heart just can't take it all in. This room, this bed that I sit on just a foot from this precious man, this place isn't the one tearing me up - it's Antonio's, Omar's, almost all of the prisoners on the other side of the grounds. As I walk to Antonio's room time and time again, each cell is entirely exposed along the way. Bars reveal the same pair of cement bunks, a few cells with shirts hanging from strings fixed to walls, a few others with bedding, but none with cooking areas, TVs, or anything else that Pedro has.

"I don't get it. It's isn't fair." I look into his deepest dark brown eyes.

"What's not fair, Maggie?" His eyes leave mine and land on his lap.

"It's not fair, period. My place then yours. Your place and then Antonio's. It's hard. It's just hard cuz we're all people; we're all just people." I try not to cry in front of him.

"Well, you have to remember that we messed up. We had a chance to be out. We've got to pay now." His eyes still find something other than me. This time it's the wall in front of him.

"What about Maelo? He hasn't even been to court yet. How can he be expected to make it here?" I am intense.

"Lots of guys in here haven't been to court. That's a system issue. It's the way it works here. It's not fun, but we have no choice." His eyes reach the floor.

"And so, you did something wrong and deserve this? Is that what you said? Do you really believe that?" A sadness comes over me. How could he possibly believe that he deserves to sleep every night in isolation, breathing in the filth that lives outside his window? How could anyone deserve this?

"Something like that, Maggie." He still can't bring his eyes to mine.

"Well, I don't think so." He continues to stare at the floor, so I gently lean my shoulder over to bump into his. "Hey," I wait for his face to turn toward mine. When he finally gives in, I meet his eyes and don't leave them.

We study each other's eyes. I know mine well, blue with a splash of green in each. His are so near black that I have to look hard to find the shade of brown that separates the inner circle from the outer. Beyond his eyes, I see a tender man with a tough exterior. He's made peace about being here on some level, but he's still really just a soul aching to be valued, just that human ache.

His voice is quieter than before, "We should get going. Marco's probably waiting for us."

"Yeah." I nod, my eyes leaving his.

I stand up and move toward the window, allowing him space to open the plywood door. He grabs his Bible, and makes his way to the main door. What is happening? Why am I so drawn to this man?

Somewhere in the middle of all this, I missed the fine line. The line that started with the awfulness that brought him here, and the line that left me on the other side.

8

later tuesday morning

MARCO WAS FINISHING UP WORSHIP when Pedro and I showed up to the prayer house.

It was our first walk through the grounds without talking.

Jorge is wearing his pink polo again today, Maelo's a no-show, and Antonio's blue wife-beater looks a little wrinkled this morning. That's all that made it to worship, a bit surprising for a Tuesday. Usually after two days without visitors, the men come early.

"Let's head to the south side and wake up a few guys!" Marco doesn't have an off button. He constantly smiles and fills silence with laughter, song, or explanations. I smile at him and move away from Pedro to have a moment with Marco on the walk over.

"Marco, I saw Pedro's ribs. They were really bruised. Really bruised. Do you think someone hurt him?" I whisper because he's just a few feet in front of us.

"Hm. I don't know, Maggie. He didn't say anything about it." Marco doesn't seem too concerned. I'm sure on some level prison fights are normal, but Pedro's a pretty good-sized guy for this place. Was there something I didn't know about him?

"Here comes your friend. Let's get him to Bible study today."

Marco loves new faces, and Omar hasn't yet warmed up to our group Bible studies.

"I'll see if I can." I'm glad to see my green-eyed friend.

Omar quickly approaches me with a kiss on the cheek, "Hey Maggie. Man, I haven't seen you in way too long." Everything he says now makes me wonder about what Pedro said. Last week he kept complimenting me, and I just couldn't stop thinking about Pedro saying he liked me.

"Really? It's been three days. I think you're just fine." I give him a little attitude.

"Three days in here is a century. Yesterday sucked. Probably the worst Monday yet." Marco quickly interrupts Omar, "Omar, basta." Whatever he told him makes Omar stop talking. I'm curious, but it's clear Marco doesn't want Omar to keep talking.

"Well, my Monday wasn't too great either. I just sat around thinking about today." I try to lighten the mood.

"Whatever. I don't buy that for one minute." Now Omar is giving me attitude.

"I'm serious!" I stare at him straight in the eye.

"Well, if so, you need to find something else to do to occupy yourself cuz that's no way to spend your time away from here." There is probably some truth to that.

Marco squeezes Omar's shoulder and invites him to Bible study. I smile and nod at him. Omar said ok as long as he didn't have to read anything out loud. How funny. Is that the only reason he sits on the sidelines or runs off to do something else every day?

We make our way to Jorge's place, just down nine or ten cells from Antonio's. Jorge is the only guy in this place who wears polos of every color. He looks too clean cut to be here. In fact, I still wonder if he was a lawyer or something before landing here. For being on the north side, his place has a lot. No plywood covering the entrance or a bed other than the slabs, but he does have a small dresser with a lamp and a stack of books. His polos hang on a line that starts on the bar of the door and stretches to a bar on the window, awkwardly dividing the room. A line made from shoelaces tied together.

We all dunk under the shirts to sit on the floor. Before I can sit down though, Jorge emerges from behind a curtain made from a bed sheet with a folding chair. He places it beside me and insists. Sweet of him.

We are in the middle of reading Acts. Pedro starts, and Marco slips out. I must have missed where he is going, but I know Pedro will do just fine. We open our Bibles to Acts 3. Omar's next to me, so I set my Bible on my right knee to let him look on. Pedro starts reading verse six. "But Peter said, "I don't have any silver or gold for you. But I'll give you…"

Before getting through it, Omar curiously asks, "So, who's Peter? What's this story about?" I smile at his childlike curiosity. I love the fact that he has no idea and has no problem asking.

"Well, Peter's a disciple. Omar, have you read the Bible before?" Pedro tries to get a feel for where to begin.

"Yeah. Well, at night I've tried." Omar waits for guidance.

"Ok. Tell me what you know – about church, about God, Jesus, anything." With that, a long Spanish conversation begins. I pick up on a few things, every time familiar words are thrown out, but mostly, I just watch the men's expressions and try to follow along.

Marco sneaks in with three men I have never seen before and sets up a small circle. They begin an intense conversation of their own.

The next six hours are spent in Jorge's room. Men laughing, smiling, talking, playing cards after awhile, just hanging out. Some normalcy in this place. The perfect Bible study welcome for Omar.

Time flies by and forces me to the thickest black door once again. Ten minutes to five, Omar and I have a moment to say goodbye. "So what'd you think, Omar? Survive your first Bible study?" I'm pretty sure I already know what he's going to say.

"Yeah, it was a surprise. I thought it'd be different. I didn't feel stupid, ya know?" His words are revealing. Behind this tough guy is another person doubting himself, held back by what life has taught him.

"I have a question. I know it's a little odd to ask you about someone else, but it's been bugging me all day." Hoping it wouldn't cause an issue, I ask, "Do you know if Pedro's been fighting with someone?"

"Fighting?" His eyes move from side to side as though he was thinking.

"Yeah." I answer.

"When? Did you see him arguing with someone or what?" Omar has no clue.

"No. Never mind." I look at the ground, knowing I will go home with unanswered questions, add this to my prayer list in the morning, and probably struggle to sleep.

"No, no, no. If you have a question, you ask it. I'll figure it out." Omar seems intent on doing anything to help me in any way.

"No, Omar. I don't want you asking anyone anything. That's not what I mean." I was getting a little uneasy now. I said too much.

"Maggie, don't worry. That's not how things work here. I don't ask about anybody. I don't talk about anybody. Nobody talks. That crap gets you in trouble. Nobody wants problems here. Here, small crap has big consequences. Everyone keeps to himself. That keeps peace. Don't go thinking I'm gonna ask Pedro or ask around about him." I could always count on Omar for details.

"Ok. I just saw some bruises. That's it." Out it came.

"Bruises? I didn't see anything."

"Under his shirt. His ribs."

"Oh, honey, that's Mondays for ya." He smiles and shrugs his shoulders like it's a given. Mondays, what in the world was he talking about?

"Maggie, it's time." Marco swipes the sweat from his neck with a towel and nods toward the guard at the thickest black door.

Omar leans in to kiss my right cheek goodbye, "See you tomorrow." I lean in to the other men, one quick kiss toward each cheek and then look at Pedro, who offers me his hand. If I wanted my cheek touching anyone's, it was his, but this man asks not.

Five o'one.

Marco walks to my side of the Bronco and opens my door, probably burning his fingers at this time of day. The Bronco is miserably hot. At least Jorge's room has a window to let in a breeze and a ceiling to prevent a heat pocket, unlike the prayer house. My jeans had soaked up the constant sweat throughout the day, but they couldn't stop my eyes from catching the sweat dripping from my forehead, then and now.

The bumpiest road takes us to paved streets, and we begin our journey home.

"Marco, why would Omar say something about Mondays?" I trust this wonderful man and know if someone can make sense of it all, it will be him.

"Mondays?" He wanted more information.

"Yes. Mondays. He said Mondays were why Pedro was bruised." I listen attentively, not sure I want an answer. And I don't. Not this answer.

"Maggie, there are so many things that you don't see, and these things, we don't need to see them. We just need to pray." His answer infuriates me.

"I want to know. I need to know, Marco. How can I pray for them if I don't know about their life?" His hesitation bothered me.

After a long pause, this man I completely trusts grabs my hand and holds it firmly in his. We ride for a few minutes hand in hand. In one sentence, what I fear becomes reality, "We don't go Mondays because Monday is the day that the guards pull out the prisoners, Maggie."

"Pull out the prisoners…" I try to prompt him to finish but I stop when I see his chin quivering. In the middle of this worn down road, this grown man is about to cry. He pulls over.

Looking straight into my eyes, he finishes, "The guards pull out prisoners. They beat them, Maggie. It's not right. They make a game of it now. It took a long time for the guys to open up to me. Antonio wasn't around for a few days last summer, and some guys told me that he was sick. I tried to visit him in the infirmary, but they weren't allowing visitors. Then he just showed up one day. He didn't talk for about a week, not a word. Back then, I had just started to meet with him. We hadn't gotten into the Bible much yet when this happened. He wouldn't open up to me. I let him have his space; I never asked. But on a Saturday, as I was getting my things together to leave, he asked me if we could pray. His first prayer request. He lifted his shirt and I saw stitches on the right, bruising on his back. He was shaking as he told me that he was scared for Monday to come. I hugged him like a baby as he shook. I asked him who, and he said five of the guards." Marco told the story with emotion aside, but I know his heart still hurts.

"So, they beat them." The words furiously left my lips.

Hearing my frustration, Marco simply says, "Since then I've seen it over and over again. Antonio's was the worst though."

"I hate them. Hate them. What's wrong with them?" I begin yelling, "Why can't the guards just leave them alone? Don't they have it bad enough? What can we do? Can't we do something, tell somebody?" My frustration hits a peak, my voice gets higher, and my tears instantly fall.

Marco grabs my hand tighter, "Maggie, I would have done something if it would have helped. It's a part of their life there. There's more corruption than you want to know about. But you can pray. We'll just take time every Monday and pray together, cover them in prayer, ok?"

I sob and nod and sob and nod. Marco holds my head against his chest, and I can feel his chest shaking, fighting tears for them, too. The rough start of the engine takes us back to the worn out road.

The fine line that justifies the inhumane. The fine line...

9

late tuesday night

THE WALLS WE WOULD LEAN up against were harsh, what they held in, harsher. The reality of so many never to see light again. The regrets of hundreds tearfully begging for forgiveness as they settle into this place. Each night, rugged cheeks meeting pillows in silence and isolation. They begged. I knew they begged. They reeked of it every morning. Pedro begged too. His long hair hitting the pillow alone, twisting, turning. It begged. For a do-over. To erase the uneraseable.

I cry at the thought of him on that pillow, and I beg too. Cry and beg for naked eyes. Eyes that never had a papa, long for that guidance, and would give anything to start over. Eyes that gave up way too long ago. Eyes that everyone else gave up on. Eyes that say *I don't matter.* Eyes that want to matter. Eyes that will never see the other side. Eyes that have seen too much on the inside. Eyes that never knew love. Eyes that will never be able to love. Eyes of regret. Eyes of denial.

Eyes stuck in the scrutiny of the fine line.

10

four days later, saturday

PEDRO'S FAMILY CAME FOR HIS twenty-sixth birthday. They brought a gorgeous cake with frosted in white and yellow flowers, quite feminine in fact. So Marco and I spent our afternoon enjoying our first sweets in this place. I could see right into his mom, much the way I can see into so many. I knew this wasn't going to be a day that she would sink into his arms and cry openly for him, but she did glance away often to stop the tears from coming. She glanced toward me with a look of thankfulness, and I saw that she was determined to be strong for him today.

"I'll be right back," Pedro opens the door with pieces of cake in his hand. As he leaves, his mom simply places her hand to her heart and breathes in. Her eyes widen, her body nearing the doorway, her arm reaching for the space he just occupied. It was then that I knew she sat as I did at night and prayed for this man, this soul... now just feet from her. Our pillows knew the wetness of tears and the heavy gasps of silenced pleas.

She turns toward me and places her hand through my hair. Marco sneaks up behind her and places his hand on her shoulder. We stand, comforting one another.

Pedro opens the door to find the three of us standing together. He looks at her, and gently takes her hand in his and places a sweet kiss on her cheek. Seeing him comfort her sends me outside for an answer to this new emotion that has never left me.

Sitting on the cement step outside of his cell, I can't stop chaotic tears from taking over, and I lose all control of my emotions. My eyes look up to a sweaty man peeking at me from behind bars, another guy with glassy eyes staring at me, men everywhere wondering why these tears fall. No privacy.

I feel this urgency to take each of these moments and plant them like seeds into a garden that I can forever see. I hear his voice. But with tears decorating my face, I can't look up. How dare I take a moment from his mother? His hand touches my back, and he gently says my name again, "Maggie." I can hear the concern in his voice. I don't want him to see me like this. His hand stays on my back as he steps down and sits with his leg touching mine. Close, but not close enough.

"Maggie." The third time was no better. Concerned, he pulls me in, and I let my head fall on his shoulder. I cry as close to him as I have ever been.

"I don't want you to be here, Pedro. It's not fair. Your mom, look at your mom. She can barely stand it here." I whine.

The quiet, "shhh" of his voice and his hand hugging my head to his shoulder soothe my gasps.

"Shhh, shhh." How could he possibly be this strong?

"Maggie, I'm going to be a better man after this." I keep my head hidden in his strong shoulder, listening to his quiet voice as my tears slow. "I made a lot of stupid mistakes. I got caught up in money and simple things turned complicated. I was trafficking. I got lost in the money, the rich life, the need to provide for my parents, my family. I thought I could give my brothers a better education, a better chance than I had."

Finally, his story. His chin rests on my head.

"The way I was living wasn't going to lead to those things. I'd probably be dead by now, Maggie. So I know it's hard to understand, but I see life here. You see what we lack, but I see that I've been given another chance to do things right. I can't screw up here. It's not around me; I don't really have a choice. I don't like it, and it took me a few years to surrender to it and realize that I wouldn't have made the right decisions on my own. I know now that the Lord gave me this time here to save me. My life will be a completely different life than the one I left." The way he makes sense of it all ministers to me.

I wipe my face to find my mascara streaked all over my palms. "I'm just a mess." I look into his eyes.

"Yes, you are." He surprises me by taking my cheeks in his hands, then uses his thumb to wipe my mascara off each cheek, and sticks a quick kiss on my forehead. His darkest brown eyes close and then something changes, as though he catches a glimpse of where we sit.

Standing up quickly, he jumps back over the fine line that constantly follows him around, leaving me on the other side.

11

the next evening

I CAN'T SLEEP. MY FACE IS hitting the pillow, but I can't sleep. He is just pounding into my thoughts. It's something about his hand and mine. It's the way that he needs someone too and can't have it. The way my dreams will be met someday and his won't. My husband will come, and I can walk around and wonder if I see his face. I can dream about the babies I'll have and know I can have them one day. Why do I lay here and think of him as if it's me, displaced? Why can't I just take him to the movies or stuff a bit of everything into a big bag and drop it off for him? Why not?

God, do You hear him? When he prays so perfectly to You, do You hear him? I can't pray like that. I don't know how to bring the whole world into a prayer, and I don't want to ever be away from him. I want to be there with him, letting him know that he is loved no matter what. Letting him know that he does matter even though he messed up. I need Your help. I don't know how to do this every day! I don't know how to be away from him and not think about him. I can't let it go. It's all I think about.

I'm so scared of Monday, Lord. I'm so scared. Not him, Lord, not him. Please, not him. Please protect him this week. Please keep the guards away from him.

I hate them. I hate the guards with everything in me. I can't even look at them; I can't stand to see their faces and think that they might be the one hurting our guys. I don't mean to hate, but I can't find any love for them. Lord, teach me to love despite what they've done. Teach me to love instead of hate. If You can use me to touch one of the guards, even one of the guards, I pray You take this hate away and use me for Your purpose. Oh, Lord, don't let my feelings get in the way. Help me fulfill Your purpose here. Forgive me for hating them. I don't want to hate them. I just can't make sense of it. Why are they out with their families? Why do they have freedom? These men break spirits, humiliate grown men, take joy in harming others. Lord, these are Your children they beat. Does Your heart hurt, too? Does Your heart bleed for them like mine does?

Let them sleep tonight. May they feel Your peace and presence this night. Please just let them rest. Just pour Your peace out on all of them, I pray. Your peace, so much more than I can give. May they take rest in You tonight. May they rest in You tonight.

It's the line that convinces you that you understand when you haven't understood a thing. The line that would never allow a tear to fall on their behalf. The line that likes it that way.

12

tuesday, early morning

There is something about Tuesdays. Different than any other day. I've come to long for Tuesdays most of Sunday afternoon and all of Monday night. A fresh coat of nail polish, hair washed and straightened, clothes laid out and ready for the cool breeze of the four a.m. Mexican air. Tuesday morning prayer never feels like an hour and a half. There's so much to cover after a few days away, I treasure this time deeply each week. Just God and me.

Mostly, Tuesday mornings are fulfilling in a way that no other morning is. The relief in their eyes as though a hint of doubt follows them every weekend. The doubt that says we might not be back, that something more enticing might captivate us over the weekend and forever sweep us away. The reassurance when we step one single step through the thickest black door. The greetings are better, the smiles bigger, the hugs tighter. Tuesday mornings.

Tuesday mornings before the fine line came to life.

Ready for Tuesday after a long weekend, I convince Marco to stop at a little tienda for liters of Coke.

While getting ready for worship, the guys pass around liters, sharing germs without a second thought. I laugh at how quickly the caffeine takes effect and brings our guys out of their shells.

Waiting to see if Pedro will show up or if I need to go get him this morning, I step out of the prayer house and look through the chain link fence to see if he's on his way. After a second or two, Marco starts strumming my favorite worship song, and the music draws me back into the prayer house, and apparently the liters of Coke draw some in, too.

Our circle expands, making room for about fifteen this morning. The bright sun blinds me as I pass along the Coke. "Yo tengo un nuevo amor, mi corazón…" Clapping fills the room and scratchy voices belt out the familiar song. Marco turns in circles shouting out an occasional, "Alelujah!" I love watching his perfectly tucked in shirt fill with sweat as he praises the Lord. Smiling, I find myself much more satisfied here than even at the tent church on Sunday mornings. Although the voices of hundreds there singing the same song is powerful, nothing grips my heart like these men, who have no other chance to worship God, to have church.

I laugh as Antonio quickly jumps off the folding table and joins Marco, now forming a duo of sorts. Bodies spinning, Antonio clapping to anything but the actual beat, and others finding as much amusement as me. Something magical happens when God shows up in the midst of filth and hears the voices of vulnerable men. Here, I belong.

With vibrant strumming and a final strong "Alelujah," Marco removes the strap from his old guitar and takes the hand towel from his back pocket to stop the early morning sweat. I blow my bangs out of my face and remove the ponytail holder from my wrist, pulling my sun-bleached curls back.

"Alright, Maggie. You ready to get started this morning? How about Maelo? Can you head over there and get him?" I nod. Marco rarely requests I go get anyone other than Pedro, but I'm happy to head to the north side.

Just past our prayer house, about twenty yards away, I see Maelo leaning on a small building with traces of once perfect light pink paint. Maelo hands a stranger something. The guy is nicely dressed, a button-up plaid shirt tucked into ironed dark jeans, shiny boots. I instinctively check for an ink stamp, but his arms are covered up. Just as I decide to head back to worship alone, Maelo waves in my direction then gives the man a firm handshake goodbye. Walking toward him, I notice him look into his right hand and put a piece of paper in his back pocket before reaching me.

With a quick kiss toward my right cheek, Maelo says, "Good morning, Maggie." His cologne is the best thing I have smelled here, so strong a scent that it sends me to a department store perfume counter back home. So many show up unshowered and unbathed that I guiltily enjoy the few who have access to every day luxuries like cologne and shampoo, but this was the first time Maelo fell into that category.

"Buenos días! Is that your family?" I softly ask as I point toward the well-dressed man. "What did you do to get in here?" My words flow out as if Maelo can process them and respond.

"Mande?" Maelo misses every word.

We pause in the walkway, stuck between two languages. We stare. I shrug my shoulders, "It's ok. Vamos." As we walk toward Marco's laughter, which is spilling out of our worship area, I feel the stares of the guy Maelo took the paper from. Something uneasy rises up within me for the first time here.

Maelo pauses and motions for me to go in ahead of him, "Marco, my goodness! I can hear you all the way down the walkway!" I smile fondly at the amazing man who lifts everyone's spirits in this place.

"Ahhhhh." Tears fall from his eyes as he catches his breath and grabs a hold of his chest. "Ahhh. Maggie. Oh, these guys. You missed it, dear." Marco takes his towel out to blot his eyes and sunburnt forehead before fully catching his breath.

"Sure! The minute I leave." I smile and capture the smiling faces of the faithful few. Maelo sits on the ground next to me, with no concern about the mound of clay-colored dirt we sit in. I, on the other hand, know sitting right here will taint my jeans the rest of the day, no patting it off.

Spanish floats about.

"Maggie, Maelo just told me that you asked him something outside." Marco translates.

"Oh, yeah. It's no big deal." I avoided the subject just in case it's not something guys choose to talk about out in the open here. I can tell by the way Maelo's hand motions in a circle that he's telling Marco it's ok for me to ask.

"What did you ask him Maggie?" Marco asks as I take a quick look at our company before putting it out there, "I asked him what he did… to end up here." I look down at the dirt that is about to blow onto my freshly painted red toenails, embarrassed by my curiosity.

Marco speaks to Maelo for a quick moment then says, "I'm going to interpret for him, ok?" And so begins our first line-by-line translation of the summer, Maelo's story.

"Well, I was accused of rape." Marco's voice repeating Maelo's words is a bizarre way to hear it.

"There was a kid down the street, a few years younger than me. He was always hanging around me and my friends." As the words come out, I find myself already uncomfortable. Was this going to turn into one of those horrible stories that made me sick to my stomach and made me hate men? I sit uncomfortably, staring into these light brown eyes, wondering what this precious soul was capable of.

"He was a funny kid, really. Not too smart, never went to school."

Maelo's eyes wander to the sky, and I see a layer of water along his bottom eyelids.

"They killed him." His voice chokes, and words I can't understand spill out of his trembling mouth.

Marco reaches toward this child, and Maelo falls toward him, a loud, "Mmmm." Pause. "Mmmm" keeps filling our space. Gasps pull his chest inward in successive breaths, over and over again. I place my left hand on his filthy sneaker and wonder why the bright red polish I wear mattered a second ago. With all the crap this kid is going through, with everything he has seen, known, heard, been a part of, been accused of, or done, why on earth was I sitting at Marco's last night painting my stupid nails? It just doesn't matter. None of it matters.

Marco embraces Maelo, maybe the first time someone has touched him, held him, in months. Maelo's memories continue to torment him, leaving his body gasping continuously. With Marco's arms holding him tight, Maelo buries his face in Marco's solid chest, his back facing me. "Mmmmmmm" Pause. "Mmmmmm." I've never heard such deep uncontrollable moans in person. The moaning of the soul when words can't describe the pain. The horrible moaning of the soul…

Antonio's large feet sway from the folding table just inches from my head, his head bowing down in respect. A few guys stand up and quietly leave the room, but most stay. Most silently stay. Stay for Maelo.

Soothing sounds from Marco's mouth begin filling the air, ever so softly, "Ah…lei…lu…jah…Ah…lei….lu…jah…Ah…lei…lu…jah…" As Marco sings, Maelo's moans increase, and we hear this child's pain, now masked by a louder "A…lei…lu…jah…" and soon accompanied by all of us, "Ah…lei…lu…jah…Ah…lei…lu…jah…"

Nearly an hour goes by before Maelo's moans fade to quiet breaths. And all that matters is that his soul can heal. Heal from what? I don't know. Maybe he begged for forgiveness that hour, not knowing that Christ hears and forgives the first time. Maybe he cried for that boy who was killed, filled with shame and empathy. Maybe he sobbed over his own life that will never be given back to him, despite his innocence. Or maybe, just maybe, he simply found himself overwhelmed in the arms of Marco, embraced on this side of the wall. Embraced where the fine line lives.

The morning that began with laughter just outside the worship area shifted to a cement ten by ten filled with grown men revisiting decisions, whether made in the midst of their full-grown years or made while mere kids.

For Antonio, Maelo's moans sent him to a place of reminiscing. "When I was ten, a guy in my neighborhood asked me if I wanted to make some money. I thought he was going to give me a couple pesos or something. Turns out, dropping off a backpack a mile down the street makes a kid a lot more than a few pesos. I ran back to his house, waited for him to get off the phone and give me my money. All I wanted was enough for a cold manzana drink from the tienda. When he filled my hand with bills, my mouth dropped open. He handed me a cold beer and told me to come back again next week. That night, I hid bottles of coke and manzana under my bed, I had over twenty bottles and money left over. When you're ten, you don't even know what to do with money like that.

"My mamá had seven kids younger than me. We didn't get even

a soda on our birthday. Never. I never went to school. I helped her. I always wanted to work like the kids who bagged groceries - a dream job, I guess. But Mamá never took us to a big grocery store like that. We walked to the little tiendas in our neighborhood. We didn't have a car. I didn't have a way to make money until that day.

"The first time my papá hit me was when my little brother found the bills under our mattress. He came running out with them. Papá started screaming and pushed me in the bathroom. I told him everything after a few hits to my head. As soon as he knew I didn't steal it, he calmed down, took me by the arm to our neighbor, and that was that.

"I started going every week, picking up a backpack, walking down the canal to a drop off, never taking a peek inside it. From then on, the guy gave Papá the money and me the cold beer. It didn't take long before Papa stopped fixing cars and just sat at home all the time. He didn't have to work.

"A couple years later, I was dealing instead of delivering. We moved into a nicer house, gate outside, everything. A big two-story house for all of Mamá's kids. Got my first tattoo the day we moved in."

The guys all leaned in, listening to Antonio's scratchy voice jump years back in time. A smile here and there, a nod every once in awhile. I sit, absorbing every detail and trying to make sense of it all. It doesn't take much to realize that the economy isn't exactly booming. All I see are people outside in the heat, hoping to have one customer, wasting a day hoping to sell something, unless they're making tortillas or another necessity. Small business here is a sophisticated way of saying "doing anything to make a buck." The city wears the mess of the economy like a casino wears neon lights.

Antonio continued, "By the time I was fifteen, I was in a gang. We were just street kids, but it eventually turned bad. I'd come home whenever, and by that point, we were okay financially. My parents didn't need me around much, and I got what I wanted. At fifteen, all you want is to hang out with friends." Antonio stopped there. But the story wasn't done. My heart just ached for him. Being used by his parents like that? How could they let a ten year old provide for them? Are you kidding me? Who would do that? I couldn't imagine, but he seems fine with it. Fact after fact. No emotion.

"So, I got mad at a guy one day, for nothing really. We fought over a stupid game. I stabbed him and ran home. I jumped in the shower and soaked my shirt, got all the blood off and ate dinner with the whole family. I didn't even feel bad. I was nervous, but I knew if he died, I'd be fine because no one saw. A couple months later, they came for me. I was sleeping and heard Papa arguing with the police. They were coming up the stairs. I panicked for a minute, but that's it. There was one witness and that's all they needed."

A few emotionless statements to sum up a life. Antonio.

"Do your parents come visit?" I quietly ask.

"The first year, yes. My mamá came to bring me things, but I haven't seen them in a few years. They have my brothers to take care of." Antonio's words tell a story of their own. This hardened man still protects his parents.

I take a long drink from my still somewhat cool water bottle, my mind spitting out questions: How could he not feel a thing after killing someone? Did he look him in the eye? Is he making it up to save face? Is he one of these guys that doesn't ever feel guilty? Why did his family stop coming? How long will he be in here? I suddenly need so many more details than Antonio gave. I suddenly need a play-by-play: Why did he have a knife? Who exactly was the guy? Why'd he do it? The missing details are weighing heavily on me and filling me with a hesitancy I haven't felt here before. How could I feel so comfortable with him all along if he is one of those guys who has no conscience?

Shouldn't there be something within me giving me some sort of clue, some instinctual red flag? Am I missing that?

Marco breaks the silence and suggests we head outside. A sudden urge to talk to Pedro comes over me, "Marco, can I grab Pedro?"

"Sure, honey. Meet us by the basketball court. We'll head there in a few minutes." Antonio's hand reaches down to meet mine, pulling me to my feet in one swift motion. I pause and realize, I'm touching the hand that touched the knife that killed a man.

It was the line that appeared before me the moment Antonio's hand touched mine.

13

later that day

BLACK IRON BARS APPEAR BEFORE me as my knuckles meet the plywood of Pedro's cell over and over again. No answer. "Pedro?" Still no answer. "Pedro?" My voice lifts a bit higher. "Pedro?" A flabby man who clearly needs a shirt makes his way toward me, motioning for me to go on in. Uncomfortably, I slowly push open the door that only locks from the outside.

"Pedro?" I softly whisper, "Pedro?" Nothing. Afraid I shouldn't be here, I make my way back outside, past the candy cart, past the entrance filled with men standing outside, lining the walls of Pedro's building. Eyes meeting mine; heads nodding for others to look at me; eyes veering away from mine, a little bit of everything.

Hopeful that Pedro beat me to the court, I walk alone to the other side, constantly aware of my surroundings. Feeling alone, completely alone.

Taking the last step from the chain links and back into the open area that houses the north side, I can see guys already on the court. A few steps further, I stop in the shade for a moment to wipe the sweat from my forehead with my tee shirt.

"Maggie..." For a moment I think I hear Pedro, but I lift my head from my shirt to find Omar's green eyes a foot from mine. "Hey." I smile, quickly pulling my tee down.

"I have to run. I started helping out in the bread bakery." His mouth says he's leaving, but his feet don't move.

Noticing the sweat from my head now decorating my tee, my eyebrows lift, "Baking bread? How'd you get that job?" We walk toward the chain link path that I just came from, my hand fervently rubbing my tee dry.

"It's a long story. I'll tell ya about it another time. I'm late!" he says like a child rushing to get to their favorite game. Omar quickly leans in and plants his lips on my right cheek, probably the only reason he stopped me before heading to work.

I glance toward the court, scanning the men for Pedro's fit physique, but he's not there, not that I can see. Perched in their windows, guys yell out as I walk by, a simple "Mayhee," an occasional "Maggie," several say "Hello," among other Spanish somethings. I have become a regular around here.

Marco sits under a skimpy tree, benefiting slightly from its shade but mostly from his straw sombrero. He pats the dirt next to him, and I take a seat.

"Marco, I went by Pedro's, but no one answered. This guy across the way told me to go in, but when I opened the door, he still didn't answer. I guess he's somewhere around here. Did anyone mention him?" I sink into my spot a little further with every word, relieved to be somewhat shaded.

"Hmm. No, I didn't ask. We just made it over here a couple of minutes before you. You want me to go back with you?" Marco sweetly offers.

"Well, he might be sick or something." I say hesitantly, knowing he would've answered me if he wanted to see me.

"Sick. Well, let's go pray for him!" Marco is already on his feet by the time he finishes his sentence, extending his left hand to help me up. Only this man could be this enthusiastic in the heat of the day. Smiling, I grab his hand, "Alright." With one swift tug, I'm back on my feet and back in the heat.

"Did you see Rogelio?" Marco asks, rather concerned.

"Who's Rogelio?" I ask curiously, knowing I had never met a Rogelio before. Definitely not in this place, and if not in this place, where?

"Pedro's roommate. I introduced you, didn't I?" Marco says confidently, although I'm sure he hasn't.

"Um, maybe. I know him. I'm just not sure if I ever met him." I say with uncertainty, wanting to leave room for error.

Within a few minutes, the line of men along Pedro's building sees my face again. We step inside and pass the candy cart, making our way to Pedro's place.

This time Marco's knuckles meet the plywood, followed by a cheery, "Pedro, mijo!" His roommate answers promptly and opens the door for us to pass through. He and Marco speak for a few minutes, then he grabs a baseball cap and waits for me to move out of the way, so he can leave. We stand in this empty space, quiet, not a sound. Just when I think we're waiting for him to go find Pedro in the yards, Marco gently knocks on the plywood door leading to Pedro's bed.

"Sí..." His voice sounds a little different, like we woke him.

"Pedro, podemos entrar?" Marco quietly asks if we can come in.

"Quién está con usted?" Pedro's voice strengthens, and I hear the springs in his mattress adjust.

"Maggie. Nadie más." Maggie - no one else, Marco gently says.

"Come in." Pedro's voice is back to normal, but walking through that door we find him anything but normal.

His right eye is lost somewhere beneath a swollen mound of purple flesh, blackening toward his nose, tears leaking from the corner of what used to be his eye. The darkest black left eye is untouched, a harsh reminder of what the other side should look like. I find myself staring, as though watching from afar, but it's right in front of me. He stands right there, a foot away, leaning heavily to the right.

"Mijo," Marco's gentle hand braces Pedro's right jaw, as our souls sink with the brutal realization.

Breathing in, Pedro tries to hide the difficulty he's having. His already bruised ribs were undoubtedly hit again, this time far worse than before. I couldn't stand to think of what he looked like under that wrinkled gray t-shirt. I couldn't stand to see him like this. I couldn't hold back the frustration or the tears and neither could he.

Marco's fatherly fingers stroke his unmarked cheek, his thumb wiping his leaking eye dry.

"I… Maggie…" Pedro's voice pleads. My two hands instinctively grab his left hand, my fingers affectionately rubbing his hand softly, attempting to soothe some part of him. My hands are the only responsive part of me. My heart sinks, my mind immediately filling with anger, making me wanting to run straight out of this place to scream at the armor on the wall, to find whoever dared to touch him and bring them to justice, to a place far worse than this, a place absent of all humanity.

My eyes close and my ears hear words, I know the two of them are talking, but I can't process it. Everything… just stops.

The line. The God-forsaken line.

His skin is warm, each of his fingers fitting between mine, holding on tightly. I open my eyes, my shocked gaze landing first on his precious face, then moving to the coffee bean color of his hand intertwined with the paleness of mine. Tears move down my cheeks, frustration wells up inside. This precious man.

"Maggie, don't cry." Pedro manages a sweet smile in my direction. He's going to comfort *me*?

Our hands stay locked as I move to kneel on the floor at his feet. Marco sits on the bed, Pedro following, "Maggie, sit up here," his quiet voice suggests. I just simply shake my head no.

There is nothing left in me. No effort to move remains. Everything seems to have been drained in an instant: my confidence in men, my quest for justice, my respect of authority, my constant desire to fight the system, my innate passion for the hurting. Drained. Instantly drained right out of me, leaving me here, on the floor of a prison cell, holding the hand of this man.

Moments of silence follow, feeling more like minutes than seconds. The three of us crammed into this little space, waiting for someone to take the lead.

"I'll be ok." Pedro isn't convincing at all.

"Did you go to the infirmary yet?" Marco asks.

A simple smile, "Nah."

Silence comes again, so I quickly slip out of the room to find something to put on his eye. I know the freezing shower water will soothe his swelling, so I look for a towel to wet.

As I pull back a thin bed sheet, which creates privacy for the bathroom, I see a blood-soaked towel folded into a perfect square sitting on an upside-down white bucket, a bucket now covered in bloody water. Reaching for the shower handle, I quickly jerk it to the right. Splashes of cold water spit sporadically out of the hole in the cement wall. Minutes later, the towel comes clean after scrubbing it against itself. I squeeze it until the towel drips clear drops down the drain.

Marco's voice floats into the shower, the two are praying. I quietly stand outside the plywood door to Pedro's bedroom, cool rag in hand, allowing them some privacy.

"Come on in, Maggie." Marco's invites.

"Ok, I'm right here." With that, I manage to open the plywood door without getting a splinter and take Pedro's offer to sit on the bed this time. Me. Pedro. Marco.

With a glance at the rag and a sincere, "Thank you," Pedro lets me know I can touch him. I just want to erase it all and make it all better. I want to let him feel the love that says it shouldn't have happened, you didn't deserve this, they had no right.

I carefully cool the place where his untouched skin meets the bruising, being as gentle as I can, gradually moving to the tender area but avoiding his swollen-shut eye. I pat ever so softly, constantly aware that his left eye is studying all of my features.

"Pedro, do you want to tell us what happened?" Marco asks.

Pedro takes the rag from me and holds it over his eye, reaching for my hand. I hold it, imagining he needs something to hold while he explains.

"I woke up yesterday morning and worked out, stopped by and talked to a couple guys. Nothing out of the ordinary." His eyes meet mine, wondering if he should go on.

I rub the tips of my fingers against his. Nothing he can say will make me feel any different about him.

"It was the 6 o'clock bed check. The horns blew. There's a rotation, and the rotation…" Pedro clears his throat, but his voice still carries a scratchiness to it, "it was our turn."

"Your turn?" I ask with a snappiness that lets him know I'm already catching on.

"Maggie, I don't want you to hear this. You aren't gonna want to come back. You're not gonna want to have anything to do with this place. Marco, she's not gonna stay." Pedro's voice breaks, he loses his composure and starts crying, falling into Marco's arms and leaving my hand empty.

Although we sit in this small room together, I feel completely alone. I watch as the man who brought me here for a one-day visit comforts the man who would trade it all for a one-day pass.

His words pierce like a cactus, poking me everywhere.

"I heard them coming in. I sat up on my bed, hoping it would be someone else this time, but my door cracked open, and I knew they were coming for me. I stood up, dropped my shoe, and when I saw that there were three, I knew I couldn't fight. The first guard grabbed my neck in one hand and shoved me past Rogelio and outside the cell. His other fist grabbed my hair, forcing my chin to the sky. A fourth guard must've been waiting outside cuz I felt hands pinning my elbows together behind my back. The one behind me tightened his grip on my hair. Two guards came at me one punching my gut, which I could take. But once he hit my ribs, he heard me gasp, and they laughed. I just remember them laughing. They took turns, nothing but my right side. Then I just saw one with a metal bar coming straight for me. I must've blacked out." Pedro turns to me, "I heard you, Maggie. I was sleeping, and I didn't know if you were really saying my name or not. I wanted to say something, but as soon as I opened my eye, I felt a rush of pain. Throbbing. Just so much throbbing in my head. I couldn't focus. I heard the door shut and knew you were gone. So, I've just been laying here. I haven't even seen myself." Pedro's voice trails off, and I bite my bottom lip, trying to do something with the fury raging inside.

"Pedro, you need to be seen by a doctor. What can I do?" Marco asks.

"Marco, I don't know how bad I am. They won't see me. I don't know. I've never hurt this bad." Pedro says with complete vulnerability.

"Pedro. No. No!" I whine, still focusing on justice, fairness, miles from the recovery mode that Marco's in. I'm bouncing from a place of clarity and redemption to all out revenge and punishment now. His hand falls on my long light curls and gets lost brushing my hair from my eyes.

I study the purple bruising, the puffy edges of what used to be his eye. I want more than anything to show this man that he is loved. So loved.

"Maggie, wait here with Pedro for a few minutes. I'm going to check on getting him to the infirmary." Marco says.

"Ok." I say, staring at this still beautiful man before me.

Why in this moment, alone behind walls, I choose to cry instead of stay strong, I do not know. Something in me aches to show him just how loved he is. And I lose sight of the battle. I fall hard and fast for the man that knows better.

His fingertips catch the first tear that falls from my eye, then he gently traces the outline of my face with his finger. He doesn't catch the next tear, or the next. But he sees them. He sees the tears that fall for him. And I can't stop myself from collapsing into his chest.

His breath suddenly heats my left cheek, leaving me looking up toward his face, our lips nearly meeting each other's cheeks, closer than ever before. My skin learns the warmth of his skin, cheek-to-cheek, feeling his skin, learning this closeness. His left hand lands gently on my back, bracing me, drawing me even closer. The moment his hand pulls me in, my mouth begins kissing his cheek. I lose all sense of who we are, where we are, and what should be. All I can feel is his touch. I kiss his cheek, ever so softly, little kiss after little kiss slowly reaching his mouth. Mouth to mouth, we meet. Motionless. Lips closed. Needing this to be more than lust, I look for his eyes.

He fails to fight back tears, saying everything without saying a word. His head drops in defeat, giving me a moment to meet his forehead with my mouth. I gently kiss his forehead and hold his head in my hands, resting my chin on his bowed head. I see his shoulders rise and feel the shake of his chest, the short breaths of the deepest cries. Here I am, thousands of miles from home, holding this man. Holding this man… holding this man.

My hand moves from the softness of his hair to his bicep, feeling the firmness of this otherwise tender man. My eyes find his eyes staring into mine, and it's but a moment when I feel his hand leave the small of my back to brush back my hair, fully accessing my face. His touch softens me, melts me right into him. Our mouths meet for the second time.

"Maggie." Pedro gently kisses the outside of my lips again, his hand constantly touching my hair. "We can't." His words say stop, but his mouth keeps kissing mine.

"Yes, we can." I whisper, afraid to pause.

"Maggie, I can't do this." Pedro leans back, bracing himself with his right hand, holding my hair between his fingers in his left hand. His eyes haven't left mine.

My heart knows exactly what he means. This could change everything. Our relationship. Our witness. Our ability to lead others. It could ruin so much: Marco's trust, Pedro's walk, my reputation.

My hand slides from his arm, rejection telling me to pull away. My instincts say something entirely different, but away I pull. "I'm sorry." I whisper, my eyes venturing from his. "I shouldn't have come."

And with those words, though I meant to apologize for coming today, I struggle to know within myself if, in some way, some part of my soul is apologizing for coming at all.

He moves his first finger to my lips and simply says, "Don't say that."

Embarrassed, I manage to say, “I’m gonna get you a cold rag, ok?” My voice is quiet, barely there.

“Maggie, hey,” he reaches for my hand, but I get off the bed and quickly push open the door to the other half of his room. The plywood door creaks to a halt, letting me know the wall completely separates us. Relieved to be out of there, I glance around for something else that will soothe his eye. Socks lay on a makeshift clothesline, and I grab one to drench in the shower hole.

Freezing water slams loudly against the peach tile and soaks the sock in a second. Bars squeak, and I step back to find Marco coming in. I turn the shower off and squeeze the sock out. “Hey!” My voice manages to come out all cheery.

“Hi honey, is he sleeping?” Marco asks with absolutely no idea of what just happened.

“I don’t think so. I just got this ready for his eye if you want to take it in.” Marco reaches for the rag and disappears behind the door. Relieved to have another moment away, I lean against the rough plywood wall.

It’s the line that tells him *we* can’t and the line that defines who can.

14

two o'clock bed check

THE BLARING NOISE OF THE two o'clock bed check wakes me from my dead stare into Pedro's shower. I don't know how much time has passed since Marco took the rag in to him, and I haven't heard a single word. The sound of another blaring air horn plummets my eardrums and brings me to full awareness. The door to Pedro's bedroom opens, and I turn to grab the handle of the cell door to avoid seeing him again. Not now. Just not now.

But it's just Marco's voice following me out, "Maggie, wait."

"Marco, what can we do?" I ask, still in a bit of a daze.

"I don't know, Maggie. I checked with the infirmary. They won't see him unless he needs stitches, and they have no report of injury." Marco manages to share without an ounce of emotion.

"Well, he needs an x-ray or something! He can't sit straight. He's practically resting his elbow on the bed cuz his side hurts so bad." The rage is stirring up within me. Am I the only one who sees this? How can Marco be so calm right now? Everything in me is screaming: Which guard? Who is staring at us walking down here, knowing what we've just seen? Which of the armor feels satisfied today?

I just want to scream at them, tell them they'll never know love, never feel joy, never be really free, never. Not without Christ. Never.

What man could beat another man and claim to follow Christ? Surely not. Clearly the armor is overlooked here. Maybe our attention has been focused on the prisoners when it should have been pointed at the guards all along. Maybe we've had our mission field all messed up. Maybe the evil in this place isn't behind the bars after all. Maybe today's sinner is masked behind the black armor.

Marco has a way of reading me. "Maggie. He's going to be ok, but something's on your heart. Something else is weighing you down."

It takes every ounce of strength I have to refocus and keep from crying. Of course I want to spill it all and tell Marco everything, every thought within me, but it's not for him to know. Not now.

Marco's arm swings around me and pulls me in for a sweaty hug. I smile, distracted for the moment. Men make their way into the dorms. There's barely anyone left on the grounds now that the air horn has blasted five times. Only five more blasts until the two o'clock bed check begins. A few guys sprint from the middle of the chain link paths, trying to beat the clock. After weeks of watching bed checks, it's clear that being late is not an option. I've never seen a man left on the grounds after seven blasts. No one takes that chance.

"Let's get him some ice and food before we leave this afternoon, ok?" I can tell Marco's suggestion is partly for Pedro's sake and partly for mine. He's right, giving him something will make me feel better. I can't even imagine leaving at five.

We make our way along the empty path to the other side. The watermelon cart is occupied by the elderly woman who checks in daily about the same time as me. Sometimes I'm first, but rarely. She opens the same faded red cooler for the guards everyday. Chunks of watermelon, already cut into perfect pieces without a single seed, four bags of ice, and a handheld metal press like my grandma uses to squeeze lemons.

I imagine her at home each night coping with the loneliness by cutting watermelon into perfect triangles, somehow feeling closer to her husband. Finding a way to serve him. Fragile she is. More fragile than any other walking in this place, even more wrinkled and delicate than the old man who sings to me from inside the infirmary fence.

I often wonder what her husband might have done to end up here. He must be eighty, maybe older. How many years has this woman walked these paths doing this same old routine? Faithful, undoubtedly faithful.

Sweet Marco greets her with a kiss on the cheek and the two exchange their hellos. I smile and study her withering hands as they dig into the cooler and fill a plastic bag with large chunks of ice. I feel for the pesos I placed in my faded blue jeans early this morning and hold up three fingers, requesting slushes for Pedro, Marco, and I. I turn around, knowing the shade is right behind me, near Antonio's window. There's not a time of day that I don't know where to find shade. Knowing it will be another twenty-five minutes before the bed check is over, I head for cover.

"Maggie, I'm going to visit for a few minutes. Do you want your slush now or on our way back?" Marco turns and asks.

"Oh, I'll wait. I'm just gonna rest in the shade for a bit. I'll be right over there." I point to the dirt closest to the building, the real dry stuff that shakes right off my jeans the moment I stand up. My mind is going nonstop. He's a prisoner, Maggie, a prisoner. He is a prisoner and you are in a prison. What are you thinking? What are you doing? Have you lost your mind?

There should be something comforting to this set up, right? Prisoners locked away in a prison, apart from society. People can sleep easy knowing the "criminal" is behind bars. But I can't help being disturbed. A soul reduced to a word?

Pedro, the drug-dealer.

What kind of life would I face if my life were summed up in one word? Not just any word, but the word that reflects my worst decision. If I had to carry that label from this day on, I don't think I could exist. And these few live out that reality every single day.

Omar, the murderer.

Maelo, the rapist.

Do they deserve it? Prisoners are nobodies after all. Too corrupt to interact with the "somebodies" of society. Locked up and isolated from the somebodies of this world.

Somebodies, the ones who cheat on their wives when the world's not watching. The ones who bully their children at home and play the flawless parent at work. The ones who mask their sin under makeup and money. The ones who claim honesty but cheat on their taxes. The sinless somebodies.

Brandy, the unfaithful.

Jill, the slanderer.

Molly, the abortionist.

Chad, the hater.

Justin, the adulterer.

Jen, the gossip.

Derek, the abandoner.

Mark, the promiscuous.

Julie, the money-hungry.

Joe, the disrespectful.

Greg, the liar.

Somebodies, the excusable.

Nobodies, the inexcusable.

Lord, I just can't see it. I just can't see it. Where's love? Where's grace? How do Your followers not give mercy? Second chances? When do You have the final say? When do Your Words become our lives?

Brandy, the forgiven.

Jill, the renewed.

Molly, the rescued.

Chad, the loved.

Justin, the redeemed.

Jen, the worthy.

Derek, the devoted.

Mark, the changed.

Julie, the ransomed.

Joe, the accepted.

Greg, the chosen.

Pedro, the soul.

Omar, the soul.

Maelo, the soul.

Have we forgotten the souls?

Or does the fine line merely erase them?

15

two thirty p.m.

MARCO INTERRUPTS MY STRUGGLING HEART with the time, "Maggie, it's 2:30, let's head over."

I open my eyes and see my favorite Mexican man holding his hand out, ready to pull me off this dirt seat. Smiling, I say, "Yeah, let's get back."

Men start coming out of the dorms, undoubtedly savoring each moment outside of their cells even if it means baking in this June heat. Watching the guys come out and fill up the space always lights up the afternoon. The bed check is always the strangest part of the day, to walk the grounds alone feels like we've stumbled into a ghost town. Watching the men fill the grounds is comforting. Heading toward the chain link paths, I can't help but wonder who did Pedro's bed check. Surely not the ones that attacked him last night.

Step after step, I continually pat my jeans, making sure my butt is clear of all dirt before being on display for every man in these walls. Marco tells me it's a given. It's unavoidable here.

Just as we step out of the chain link fence to the open area that leads to Pedro's, I see Pedro's roommate heading our way.

"Buenas tardes, Rogelio." Marco says.

"Buenas tardes." Rogelio quickly begins a full-blown conversation with Marco that I can't follow. I don't know if this is about the incident, but I'm pretty sure it is, and I just can't be left out. "Marco," I finally interrupt.

"Yes, Mags." Marco pauses and Rogelio steps back, making room for me to join in.

"I need to know. I'm dying here, please?" I beg for the very details I know will make it even worse. Why Pedro? Who had the nerve? Or do I want to know every detail?

After taking a minute to tell Rogelio to wait, Marco starts, "Ok, Honey. Rogelio said after the beating stopped, he and Pedro were the only guys not locked in their rooms for the night. They left Pedro bleeding on the cement, so Rogelio grabbed a blanket off Pedro's bed and laid it on the floor beside him, rolled him on to it, and dragged him into their room. He said he wasn't conscious while he dragged him or most of the night. But he constantly checked his chest to make sure he was breathing. He got him off the floor and on to his bed then started washing the blood from his face. He said there was just a deep cut on his right eyebrow and his nose was still bleeding."

"Then what?" I need details.

Marco carefully translates Rogelio's every word for me. "I grab a bath towel and get it wet, dabbing the blood from his hairline and down his neck. The whole time, I check his breathing. I'm so scared he will die right there. I say "Pedro" a hundred times. He never answers me. He just breathes.

"I hear the guys next door yelling something, and I'm scared to answer. Everyone else is quiet all around us. Usually people are playing cards or watching their TVs and there's noise all around. Not last night. Nothing. You see something like this, and you know it could be you, and you get scared, and you don't do anything but lay there. You give respect to the one who got it.

"But the guys next door keep saying something until I ask them what's up. They tell me that the guards are gone. I don't know what to do. I never had to fix somebody up. You understand me? I know he's gotta breathe. That's all I know.

"The guy next to us, Carlos, he keeps saying stuff just loud enough to hear him. He tells me to look under his clothes. I lift his shirt and see it's bad, ribs sticking out and all this crap. All on the right. I tell Carlos and he says lay him on the other side. I push his chin down like my mama told me to do to my baby so it wouldn't choke at night. Thought maybe he'd vomit or something.

"He started shaking a lot this morning. Shivering. The first time I hear him moan, I know he's going be ok, come out of it. He's making noises. I yell over to Carlos and he tells me to get blankets on him, so I grab my sheets and a few shirts to cover him. He's shaking everywhere. I was afraid to touch him cuz I don't know where he's hurting. His eye was so bad, worse than now. It was so swollen. I couldn't see his eye at all. He was moaning and I say, 'Come on, man. Pedro,' over and over but he never answers. I sat next to him and stared out the windows listening to the stupid chickens wondering why they had to do it." Rogelio looks at me for the first time and gives me a forced smile.

"Who was it?" I naively ask.

Marco asks him, but all Rogelio does is stare. No answer.

"So we just sit here and do nothing?" My rage begins to show itself in my tone, "That's what we do? We sit and do NOTHING?"

Marco's hand meets my shoulder, and I coldly shrug it away. He looks at me with patience, unoffended.

"Mags," he waits for me to look at him, but all I can do is shake my head no.

Not fair. Not okay. Not going to let this go. Not Pedro.

"Maggie," Marco says again, slightly more insistent. I bite the pieces of skin around my nails and peek at him through the hair Pedro touched an hour ago. My eye contact serves as my only reply.

"Maggie, they can't fight this battle. They won't win. It's a game, and there's no other option. You play, and you lose, that's it. If we complain, we complain to the game makers. The warden? He knows. The other guards? They won't stop it. Even the decent ones, they won't stop it. The government? This is the last thing on their list. It's a part of life here. All we can do is pick up and move on." His words come out so smoothly they feel rehearsed, as if I should quietly concede.

Not this girl.

"Rogelio, how often does it happen?" I have to know more.

"Every Monday but not usually this bad." Marco translates.

Not usually this bad. So we've got hundreds of prisoners in four dorms. Hundreds of cells and plenty of guards. Then we have Pedro, messed up a couple of weeks ago and then again last night? It's not making sense. If they only target a few guys each week, then why him again?

"Why Pedro? Why not you?" I ask Rogelio, expecting a real answer and surprised to get a thorough one.

"Pedro used to be untouchable. He was a dealer. The guards knew it. They let him deal and he hooked them up. Went on his whole first year like that. Guys in here knew he was in good with the guards, so they didn't dare mess with him. The guards had it easy. Drugs for nothing. They let the middleman bring the drugs in. No questions. Word is the middleman didn't show up one day. Not the next day. A week went by. He never came again. A friend of his came one day and said he was found dead in his front yard, beat 'til he died. Kids and wife screaming right inside the house.

"When it all stopped here, no one said anything. It was just like everything else. No one says much. No one complains or goes looking for you. People adapt and go on to the next thing." Rogelio just keeps talking as though he's had this all stored inside of him for too long.

"It was bad for Pedro though. Nothing left with the guards, no loyalty from guys here. The guards treated him like they treat all of us but worse. The first month they got him pretty bad. I watched the whole thing. They thought they could get him to talk. Kicked him, smacked him, wanting info. He would've talked if he had anything to say. I know he would've. You don't live here and protect the outside.

"The next whole year his parents came almost every week. Built the walls in our place. Made their presence known. Took almost a year for him to become one of us. He got his mind off selling his way out of here. Pedro's a dreamer and no one can dream in here." Rogelio's words fill in a few gaps, but nothing makes yesterday make any sense.

Is he selling again? There's no way. He doesn't even look at the guards. Nobody stops by. I spend nearly every day, all day, with him. So why him? Why after all this time?

"I don't get it, Marco. Ask Rogelio what's going on now. That was all a few years back." I have to keep going.

"I don't know." Rogelio's eyes meet Marco's but not mine.

I can't help but gaze at the armor, posed high above the ground. Black uniforms decorating these lifeless walls, sucking the very life from everyone beneath. An ever-reminder that the power lies in the black armor, in their guns, in the authority to shoot on demand or on a whim. We're the specks below, able to be blown away at any moment if the armor sees fit. An ever-present reminder stationed on the walls.

My nerves run deeper as my eyes leave the armor and look ahead to the path that's just moments from Pedro. The plastic bag is already slushy and the watermelon slushes are liquid already.

"Marco, let's get this stuff to Pedro before it melts." My voice is quieter now, a reflection of my mood change, my attempt to understand every aspect of this side of the wall, pleasant or not.

"Yeah. Give me a minute to tell Rogelio we're going to stay with Pedro until we go home." Marco turns to Rogelio, and I sip my watermelon drink, wondering how I'm going to face Pedro in his cramped cell.

A few steps closer. Marco's familiar arm swings around my back and lands on my shoulder, "It's going to be okay, Maggie. It's always going to be okay. You know better now how to pray for him. We will pray together for exactly this, for every Monday, and the Lord will heal him. Pedro has a life ahead of him, Maggie, and we don't know what he must learn in here or why he must learn it." Marco's words don't sit well with me. I am far too upset to see the good in this.

I want to shout back, *Really? What was that supposed to mean? Thank God he got beat so I can learn how to pray? There are other ways to learn lessons! This wasn't of God. This wasn't some complicated spiritual intervention to change Pedro's path in the future. This was evil. God is not responsible for sin. Ever. He can't be the source of it. Ever.* Oh, how I want to scream it all and challenge everything, but I know precious Marco knows all of it already, and I know he means well.

I don't say a word.

I just nod and smile and look at the man who chooses to spend his days here instead of anywhere else.

Here. Of all places.

Marco approaches Pedro's room first, knocks firmly, and calls out, "Pedro?" I'm shocked to see Pedro's hand pulling the door open. Part of me wants to turn and run out of here, and the other part wants to run right in there and hold him.

Marco takes a step into the room and pauses to hold the door open for me, "Maggie, come on in, Honey." I wonder if Marco can see the struggle hiding behind my smile.

The moment I step into his room, I can tell he's looking right at me. I'm instantly fighting back tears. I have no idea how to look at him and be okay. I feel the tears rush to my eyes, and I try to avoid them by taking the bag of ice from Marco. I manage to grab one of the last solid pieces of ice and carry it over to the counter. The silence within these walls is killing me. My hands burn from the cold. *I'm so stupid. Why did I let myself? He doesn't even care.* I find a yellow tinted grocery bag and stick the ice in it. It's the size of an apple, perfect for his eye. I tie the bag in a knot just above the chunk of ice and stare at the wall. *Turn around. Just turn around.*

Before I have a chance, I feel a hand on my arm. *Please don't let it be Pedro.* The simple touch sends quivers up my arm, and I know it's him. "Thanks, Maggie," Pedro's says as his hand reaches for the ice pack. My eyes find his and my mouth says an inaudible, "Of course."

More silence.

I turn and face Marco, who has taken a seat on the bare mattress. I watch him rub the sweat from his forehead, the wet rim of his sombrero resting on his knee. Pedro uses a book to prop open the door to his bedroom, allowing the window fan to bring in a breeze. It feels as cool as it's felt all summer in the middle of the day. The only time I feel cooler air is in the middle of the night in Rosie's room when darkness caters in a cool breeze.

"Sit down, Pedro. You don't need to be walking around." My voice comes out this time, ever so gently. I watch Pedro try to sit next to Marco, squinting with pain, unable to find a comfortable position. I can hardly stand it. I want to fix him, find something that will heal him, and find some real nurse that doesn't need an incident report before looking at his ribs. He lets his right arm rest on his leg and uses his left arm to hold the bag of ice over his face.

In front of us. Everything in front of us.

I look at him. This full-grown man. Bruised. Swollen. Aching. It's in this moment that I know I can't turn away.

My feet stop just before his, my knees bend until they reach the floor, and I kneel down, my head a foot from him. It's there that I place my hands on his knees and pray through my tears.

"God, I pray You place Your hands on Pedro now. God, we don't know what to do. No one will help him. He's hurting and he's a mess and we have nothing. God, we need You. We need Your hands to touch him and heal him in the way that only You can. God, I don't understand why this happened, and I can't help. I pray You give him the strength to care for himself tonight. Lord, watch over him. Please don't let them do this again. I can't... I asked You. I asked You to protect him." My voice breaks.

Pedro's hand covers mine.

Bawling now, I sink my head down to my feet and let go of his hand, completely lost for words. I try to stop my shoulders from moving, from showing how the crying has overtaken my body. Completely lost. Until his strong voice takes over:

"Father, I give Maggie to you now. Lord, touch her sweet heart. Show her Your ways. Let her feel Your peace tonight. I thank You for bringing her here. Her smile is a ministry to us all. Father, refresh her tonight for her work here tomorrow. May this not be a distraction for her. Father, I know You are here with us. We thank You for another day." Pedro's firm voice gets louder and more determined. *"God, we need Your power to move on us, to heal us, to teach us Your ways and to see Your good even in here."*

I feel hands touch the top of my head, and I hear Marco join in, two voices now, but their words don't register anymore. I lose all concern with how I'm shaking, what's dripping down my face, and where I am.

I simply breathe in a peace, breath after breath. Peace and more peace, a sweet, soothing peace.

And I rest.

In His peace.

His sweet, sweet peace.

God, who takes me beyond all lines.

16

the next morning, four a.m.

I CAN'T SLEEP. I'VE NEVER CRIED to the point that I couldn't pray. I've never heard the weak pray for the strong, and I've never thought to thank God as if this could be my last day. Never. But I have felt the peace of God before.

The window fan brings in the cool breezes of the night air and slightly moves my thin bed sheet. I suddenly miss nestling under blankets in an air-conditioned house and hot shower water nearly burning to the touch - instant relaxation. My mind keeps tossing around the every day luxuries that never were luxuries. The convenience of drinkable water coming out of faucets and no hesitation to rinse my toothbrush or use as much toilet paper as I like and flushing it rather than folding it up for the waste basket. A fridge packed with excess: yogurt, fruit, cheese, lemonade, juice, sodas… a pantry. An actual pantry to stock up on food. Not here.

Here are fresh tortillas each day from down the street and a weekly stop for groceries, groceries that might feed two in the States somehow stretch to feed six here. I live for these nightly breezes and thank God I brought tight knit shorts to wear under everything to stop the constant sweat. The sticky hot seats of our Bronco, the debate between what's more refreshing - sitting outside to catch a midday breeze or sitting inside, blocked from the sun but trapped with the heat…?

I hear the sound of Marco snoring, a steady, predictable snore just outside my bedroom, and I know his alarm will wake him up in a few minutes. I wonder what today will be like.

I wonder if Pedro even wants to see me. What did he mean, we can't? We can't *what*? We can't kiss? We can't be seen? We can't be together? We can't get close? We can't touch? We can't fall for each other?

Did he feel instantly convicted? Why didn't I?

Is he awake right now wondering what to say to me?

Does he even care?

I'm such an idiot. How have I gotten to this point? Just weeks in and I've fallen. What is it that I can't shake? What is it that I'm missing? Why can't I just see the prisoners, minister to them, leave and shut it off? Why do I take them everywhere I go? What am I doing wrong? I am so far-gone, stuck in this world of wrongs.

I just want to hold him, let him know that he is loved, so loved. Loveable, so loveable. I didn't mean to kiss him. I didn't plan it. I just wanted him to know that I care. That, somehow, someway, this prisoner with a messed up past in a filthy prison has so much to give, to love, and to share. That he is worth so much more than the way it appears. That I can see it. People are out there who can see it.

I don't even know if I should be here anymore. Marco shouldn't have invited me to stay. I'm screwing up everything. I don't even know Spanish. I can hardly speak a word, and I sure have no idea what they're talking about most of the time. I'm making everything take longer than it should. Every Bible study is translated now, so we don't get as far, as though I matter enough to take from them. This ministry is for them, and I'm messing that up. I'm a distraction to half the guys. They're coming to see a girl. Omar was right. They're not coming to hear the Word. I have no idea what I'm doing here.

I stare at Rosie sleeping under her covers, so acclimated to the heat that she's chilly. I see her and wonder if it's time to go back home. Maybe I don't belong in this environment after all.

The fine line lives in so many places.

17

wednesday morning

A LITTLE BOY STARTED CHASING OUR Bronco last week. Every time we hit the dirt road that leads to the prison, he is waiting for us to show up. It must be his morning entertainment, his run in the nude entertainment. He doesn't have underwear or shoes, never a shirt or shorts. Just a naked skinny brown body and the most determined little racing pose I've seen.

Today, Marco pulls over just as we make the turn on to the road.

"Do you want to come with me, Mags?" Marco surprises me.

"Um, ok. Where are we going?" I look around, clueless about Marco's plans.

"I'm going to stop and visit here."

"I'd love to come!" I jump out of the Bronco and follow Marco.

The poles that hold up sheets and tarps look like the poles used in the chain link fences. They're just sticking out of the ground holding up nearly every fabricated home here. I watch Marco lean close to the sheets and politely call out, "Señor? Señora?" at tent-house after tent-house. After a brief conversation with a young girl dipping her baby in a bucket of water, he points over to the tent-house next to the street.

"She knows our little friend. His name is José. The house with the blue tarp." My eyes go straight to the place that's even smaller than Pedro's room, and sure enough, there he sits.

I squat down, "Buenos días, José." Our ornery little friend is actually rather shy this morning.

His big brown eyes look right at me, then he draws a circle in the dirt. I try another hello, "Hola, José." Then I look up at Marco.

"Dónde está tu Mamá, José?" Marco asks for José's mom, and with that, he jumps his naked self up and walks. We follow the little guy and watch him tug on a dress and say, "Mamá." The prettiest girl turns toward us and meets Marco's cheek with hers.

The two talk for a few minutes while I squat back down and draw a car in the dirt for José. I finally get a smile and watch him copy my car, line for line. We play draw and copy, draw and copy until Marco says, "Mags, are you ready?"

"Sure." I stand up and wave a little goodbye to the boy with no clothes.

"Maggie, this is Ivon, José's mother." Marco introduces us.

"Hola!" I smile at the girl who must be younger than me. She steps toward me and offers me her cheek. We greet, and I leave as quickly as I came.

I wait until Marco starts the Bronco and gets back on the road before asking why we stopped.

"I just wanted to introduce myself. She has four little boys. José's the oldest." Marco says.

"The oldest? But he looks so little!"

"He's six," Marco smiles. "Six, four, one, and a new baby."

"What? She looks so young!" I'm completely shocked.

"I didn't ask her how old she is, but it looks like she is rather young. We'll pick them up for church tonight." Just like that, Marco reminds me that our work is never finished.

We pull up to the familiar rock-filled parking lot. I slip my water bottle over my shoulder, and Marco grabs his guitar and his bag filled with ice. We head up to the doors. Feeling refreshed, I look at each guard, get my ink stamp, do my bag check, and step in for my full-body check. I wait for Marco to come out of his closet.

"Ju Pedro girlfriend?" I turn my head quickly and see the guard who just gave me my number looking at me.

"Me?" I look right at him. He speaks broken English. After all these days of playing me, he can speak if he really wants to. A brief nod of reassurance answers me.

"No. No, I am not with Pedro. No Pedro. No girlfriend. I am *friends* with Pedro." I notice that I'm squinting and getting a little defensive.

He just nods and nods, looks me up and down and nods. I feel sick to my stomach having him look at me. I want to go inside and find the guys and be surrounded by people that know me. His cold stare doesn't stop. I decide to walk out of his range and wait outside for Marco to finish. What's taking so long?

I can't get my mind off of his question. That guard is never on the other side. He sits in the same place giving out numbers and collecting numbers every single day. How does he even know Pedro and why would he think I'm with him? I'm contemplating going back in there to ask him, but I feel so self-conscious after being looked at like I'm one of the "regulars" here, that I can't move. I look down at my dark jeans, brown flip-flops, just a simple light t-shirt, bright yellow, no jewelry at all, just bright pink nail and toe polish and a little lip-gloss and mascara. I'm so tan and often sunburnt that my skin's all dried out and slightly freckled. There's no need to wear hardly any makeup here, definitely not as much as the "regulars." My hair-tie is wrapped around my wrist just like every morning. It sits there until I can't stand the weight of my hair adding to the discomfort of the heat.

I know I don't look like them. The ones who walk in here every day, barely covering their breasts, wearing pants that look painted on, shirts skin-tight even if that means their fat is spilling out. Why is he treating me like one of them?

I can count the number of times that I've been inside Pedro's room alone. Two. Once when Rogelio let me in and yesterday morning. The first time was only a minute or two, yesterday was just a little while. I don't understand why he thinks I'm one of them. A prostitute?

He thinks he can look at me like that. He looked at me and knew I was watching him look me up and down, as though it was okay with both of us.

Sick. I look ahead, walk off the path and lean over, afraid I'm going to puke. My whole body feels instantly sick, and I wish I had some sort of blanket to wrap around me. Something to cover myself up with.

"Maggie?" Marco appears behind me. I stand up, meeting him with fear in my eyes.

"Honey. Hey, Maggie…" It's now that I cry, right here in this place as though I have absolutely no control over my emotions. And I'm angry I'm even at this point. One little comment from one guard is breaking me down. Why am I letting myself break?

Marco sets his guitar and bag down and holds my face in his hands, "What is it, Maggie?" His gentle voice comforts me.

"The guard that gives our numbers" my voice trails off, and I breathe in slowly to stop myself from crying.

"He asked me if I was Pedro's girlfriend." I look at Marco, expecting the same anger to rise up in him, but it doesn't.

"Oh, Honey," his hand meets my chin, "Honey, look at me." With that, my eyes meet his in total trust.

"Do you remember prayer this morning?"

I nod.

"What did Pastor Jorge say? Did you understand him? Maggie, we wrestle against demons and principalities. Our war is not against man. If Satan can upset you before you walk through those doors right there, then what has he done? He's wounded you so you can't do what God wants today. He will depress you, confuse you, make you question everything. He will mess with your mind to keep you from ministering today." Marco's words are exactly what I need to get my focus back on our mission.

Nodding, I simply say, "Ok, I've got it."

Smiling, Marco kisses my forehead and reaches down for his guitar and bag. I follow him to the thickest black door.

One single step through. I feel for the small white piece of paper that labels me number sixteen and push it to the bottom of my back left pocket until it's snug. Then I turn back and look straight into the guard's eyes. Today I will study each one of them. Today I won't avoid the armor. I'll look at them without hesitating. I'll face the cruelty behind this side of the wall.

Antonio is the only one waiting for us today. He quickly jumps up off the ground and grabs Marco's guitar, his bag, and my water bottle, happy to carry things for us. I can't do anything but smile at his helpfulness. His hair is nappy today, clearly not washed, his blue wife beater still showing yesterday's sweat stains. I wonder if Victor would let me bring him one of his shirts tomorrow. Or maybe I can bring his shirt home to wash, or would that would be insulting? He doesn't seem to mind wearing it every day.

"Let's go to the prayer house this morning." Marco tells me as I hold on to his shoulder to walk through the chain link pathway. Just a ways away, I can see my morning greeter, but this morning he starts shouting out the song made just for me even before I reach his fence.

"Maaay - heeeee… Maaaaaaaaaayyyyyy HEEEEEEEEE, ju eyes

bee tee ful, oh. Oh, Maaaay – heeeeee" Unless he sings to me in Spanish, it's this same song daily, using every English word he knows, loud and clear for the prison to hear. I smile at him and touch his fingers that stick through the chain link fence. His scratchy loud voice accompanies us along the path, an expected part of the routine here.

The prayer house is empty this morning. It must've been a late night. The three of us sit on the folding table and wait for awhile, Marco contagiously laughing at a seemingly hilarious Antonio. I can't help but join in, even though I have no idea what's funny. They keep going, but I, I just stare. I'm distracted being in the prayer house just minutes away from Pedro. I'm too close to not see him.

Where is he? Does he want to see me? All the thoughts from this morning are still running through my mind. What did he mean when he said, "We can't?" I need time with him to say I'm sorry. I never should have. I know better. In all my days here, with all the prayer, never once did I mean to mess things up. I never meant to do any harm. I got caught up in the moment. I didn't want him to hurt. I wanted him to know that I see so much in him, even here.

"Ahh, Maggie, this guy is cracking me up!" Marco looks toward me, still laughing.

"I can see that. Goodness, you two." I smile, distracted for a moment.

"Ok, well, if no one else is coming, let's get this ice to Pedro before it melts." Marco stands up, grabs his bag, and reaches around Antonio's shoulder, pulling him in close, one more moment of laughter.

Just as we make our way into the pathway, Rogelio shows up wearing saggy burgundy jeans and a once white undershirt.

"Hola!" He greets each of us and begins walking with us toward their place. He doesn't stop talking to Marco the entire three or four minutes it takes to go through the chain link maze, head through the open yard, and wind up inside the plywood door.

Pedro's not sitting in the open room, and I don't hear the sound of water beating against tile, so I'm sure he's resting in bed.

"Maggie, Rogelio said Pedro asked him to come find us this morning. He would like to see us and have prayer in here. I've invited Rogelio to stay. Get comfortable. Go ahead and take a seat. I'll go back and check on him." Marco gently opens the door to Pedro's bedroom.

I find myself relieved to be in this part of the cell instead of staring straight into his eyes. He wants to see me.

I don't sit. I stand, still scared to see his eye, and even more afraid of not knowing what to say especially if we don't have a minute alone. Butterflies start taking over my stomach, nerves creep in everywhere. Pedro's familiar voice leaks into the room, but his Spanish is too fast for me to follow. I'm dying to know every word he says.

"Maggie?" Marco loudly calls, wondering if I can hear him.

"Yeah?" I answer.

"Can you bring in the ice? Find a bowl or something for some of it to fit in his freezer, make an ice pack or two?" I panic. I hope his eye isn't worse this morning, I can't imagine it being any more disfigured.

"No problem. Just give me a minute." I look around the room and find four yellow-tinted grocery bags folded into perfect squares peeking out from underneath a washcloth. Rogelio stands up to help me, not knowing what Marco asked me to do. I open up the mini-fridge and see that the freezer is only a few inches tall, so I decide to divide the ice between the four bags and cram three into the freezer to stay frozen. Half of the bag of ice is already melted, so the three bags will conform to the freezer just fine. Rogelio holds a bag open for me, and I grab the largest chunk of ice for Pedro's ice pack. I tie a knot in the bag above the chunk of ice.

Antonio jumps up off the bed and reaches for the bag. I smile at this tattooed mural, a stark contrast from the child within, and gladly let him take it to Pedro.

Antonio disappears behind the bedroom door, and Rogelio and I get the other ice packs put into the freezer. I flatten the ice bag we brought and fold it up, placing it under the washcloth. I look at Rogelio, neither one of us able to say anything to the other.

Grateful to hear the sounds of the hinges creaking, I turn around and see Marco coming out of the bedroom.

"Maggie, Pedro will be out in a second." Marco reassures.

"How is he today?" I ask, a part of me envying the moments Marco just spent with him alone.

"He's doing good. He's more sore than yesterday, but he's alright. Antonio is helping him get dressed."

"Good." I smile, nerves rising once again.

We all stand in silence until Rogelio reaches for the worn gray blanket on the shelf above the bed and puts it over the peach tiled floor.

"Let's all sit on the floor and give Pedro the bed to lay on. It's pretty hard for him to sit up." Marco suggests.

I wince at the thought of his pain, ribs poking out toward his skin yesterday, shards of bone noticeably out of place.

Antonio comes through the door, Pedro close behind him. He's hunched over, not able to stand up straight, still leaning heavily toward the right.

Time hasn't healed his face at all. The swelling seems worse than yesterday, black marks now reaching over his nose and to the left side, purple bruising expanding to his left eye today. His right eye isn't visible at all. There's nothing but a mass of swollen skin covering his entire eye socket in an array of purples. Areas of dried red blood still stain his forehead. His cheekbone is now defined because it's protruding abnormally, another apparent target for the guards.

His oversized jersey hides everything else, everything but his pride, lost in this place.

I look at him and lose everything I carefully planned up to this moment. I know that as much as I want to believe that I can be strong and apologize for getting too close and assuming too much, that I will not be able to. For in this moment, I see the man whose cries I know, and my soul aches once again. I know I can't lie to him, and I'm not sure if I really am sorry.

The only one left who hasn't said hello, I step toward Pedro, and say a simple, "Good morning."

He offers me his hand, "Good morning, Maggie. Good to see you." He pauses, still holding my hand after I let go.

"Lay down, mijo," Marco helps Pedro get situated on the bare mattress. Nobody besides me seems to mind that it's missing a sheet.

"Well, I want to open up with our study this morning. We're in Acts, chapter eighteen. Maggie, you can use my Bible. I'm going to read in Spanish for Antonio and Rogelio, just follow along." With that, I take his side-by-side Spanish/English Bible and begin reading the verses to myself in English.

Sitting next to Antonio, I can't help but notice his constant bouncing knee, his energy barely containable, but he does stay focused on Marco's every word. We stop in verse nine and ten where God speaks to Paul in a dream. "Do not be afraid; keep on speaking, do not be silent. For I am with you, and no one is going to attack and harm you, because I have many people in this city. So Paul stayed in Corinth for a year and a half, teaching them the word of God."

Antonio blurts out the obvious, "God promises to protect Paul for teaching people the Bible."

"That's right, Antonio, he does. That's exactly what He does." Marco responds.

"What else are these verses saying?" Marco asks.

After a minute of silence, I say, "He tells us He is our protector, that there isn't anything to be scared of when we're spreading the message of Christ."

Marco translates for the guys, then I add, "Like when I come here. We pray every morning from four thirty until six o'clock, and I walk in here with confidence each day, never scared, never afraid, I always feel God's presence." Marco finishes translating for me.

Antonio looks up at the sky, almost looking distracted. He surprises me when he says, "Marco, I don't understand."

We all look at him. "How come God didn't protect Pedro? He teaches the Bible." My heart sinks at the simplicity of Antonio's question.

"Antonio, that's a good question. Now, did God protect Paul all the time, or is this verse just talking about Paul's time in Corinth?" Marco has a way of being very careful when teaching Antonio, aware of his childlike mentality.

"I don't know." Antonio answers.

I spend the next hour listening to Marco explain the many trials Paul endured, along with the many miracles. Marco answers everyone's questions carefully and thoroughly, and spends a lot of time on what God's plans are for our lives.

As they continue talking, I take a minute to switch out Pedro's melted ice pack for another one from his freezer. He puts the new one on his ribs and props himself up, now sitting on the bed.

After watching the guys sit and talk, I ask Marco if I can go buy some tacos for the group.

"You have money, Maggie?" he asks.

"Yeah, I have some cash, well, a five dollar bill." I watch Marco add it up in his head.

"I think they're about four for a dollar here, a lot cheaper than out on the street," he answers.

"Ok, I can go." I'm anxious to get out of the circle of Spanish.

"Give me a minute to see if everyone's ok with that." Marco says.

"Alright, it looks like the guys would love that. It'll be five sacks of four. You know what, I want to see if some of the other guys are wondering where we are. Why don't Antonio and I head over there, and you can stay here with Pedro and Rogelio?" Marco says exactly what I want him to say, but now I feel sick to my stomach once again. The thought of being here with him leaves me uncertain, scared, too vulnerable.

I pull the bill out of my dark jean pocket and had it to Marco. He plants a quick kiss on my cheek, "See you in a little while, Honey."

Plywood meets metal. I stand, almost alone with Pedro. I immediately turn away from him and busy myself with flattening the first ice pack and folding that sack. I stare at the cracks in the cement wall in front of me.

"Maggie, don't worry about that." Pedro says with sincerity.

Intentionally staring at the indentations in the cement, I continue to fold the sack. Once again, my eyes fail me, creating tears despite my determination to hold it together.

I see Rogelio slipping out the door quietly. Now what do I do?

"Maggie? Maggie, don't make this difficult. Don't make me come over there." Pedro teases.

"In that case..." I try to talk without letting him know I'm crying.

I wipe under each eye, breathe in deeply, and breathe out, turning toward him.

"Maggie...hey..." he immediately notices and his voice sinks.

I feel my lower lip shaking, and I try to fake a little smile, but my tears are already coming. I can't hold them in, not for even a second. Not able to hide an emotion from him, I sit next to the man who knows what's going on.

"Are you still upset about yesterday?" He adjusts his ice pack and scoots back a little to see me.

"I don't know what you expect me to say, Pedro. Of course I'm upset." I pause for a minute to breathe and gather strength before making eye contact.

"I have no idea what you're thinking. I don't even know if you want me here. You have no idea what yesterday is doing to me. Part of me just wants to leave and go back home. And part of me wants to sit here with you whether or not you want me to." I say everything I want to say without stopping. It all spills out, tears, quivering lip, and all.

My eyes move from his eyes to his knee, just an inch from mine. I fixate on his black jeans, not daring to see how he's processing everything I just blurted out in my raw emotion.

I wait.

The dark skin of his hand lands on his knee, his fingers bouncing anxiously on his knee. My eyes leave his fingers, travel up his arm, and stop on his shiny black jersey, a bit closer to his face.

I wait.

Then he says what I haven't even considered, "Maggie, there hasn't been a girl in my life that I've watched and respected from afar. Every girl I've known, every girlfriend I've had, they've all been pretty short-term, nothing meaningful. Not one."

Concentrating on the place where his jersey meets his neck, still unable to meet his eyes, I carefully listen to his every word.

I wait.

"I've never kissed a girl that I care about like I care about you. I don't want to treat you like everyone else. I don't know what to do with you. I'm scared to touch you."

The moment my eyes look for his, his close.

Of all the possible things that Pedro could say at this moment to leave me speechless, this was by far it.

Waiting for his eyes to meet mine, I cry tears of a new kind, tears sparked by his openness. Tears I've never known before. Tears I may never know again.

I touch his knee, causing his eyes to finally meet mine.

"Good enough." I tease through tears.

"Oh, that was good enough?" Pedro laughs, "I pour my heart out to you and I get 'Good enough'?"

He looks right at me, assessing my response.

"Could've done better." I tease.

"Oh really? You think?" Pedro says, as our hands instinctively grab a hold of each other's.

My tan fingers look pale between his. He lifts my hand and kisses it firmly, leaving it to rest on his lips for a moment.

The fine line between what's close and what's too close.

18

the following monday

It was Pedro from the very beginning. Something in his eyes was too pure to be here. Something in his words was so true and transformed, leaving no trace of a jagged past. He told me his story. I told him mine. He had a way of placing his arm innocently around my back to walk through the yards, my shield.

Pedro filled my thoughts at night and led my laughs all day. Just my fingertips brushing along his arm without him flinching or the way he didn't hesitate to smile the moment I stood in front of him were breakthroughs. Weeks ago, neither one would have happened. We learned a new close. It wasn't a night of passion or a freight of lust. It was the simplicity of our interaction that left me longing for time with him, something pure, something intense.

Our goodbyes at the thickest black door were unlike the others. Their cheek kisses were brief. Our hugs were long. Our lips never met each other's cheeks, but our faces would press tightly together, allowing his cheek to feel the warmth of another cheek, my hand holding his face tightly to mine. He let me near him in so many ways. I began to love being held in his strong arms, my head fitting just below his chin. I let the warmth of my breath land on his neck, on the neck that hadn't known a woman's touch in years. On the neck of the man who took me in and taught me the ropes. On the neck of the man who never asked for my affection.

The fine line. I couldn't see it. Somehow others could. Mom spoke of the line frequently during rare phone calls. Even Marco could remember the line. The guards lived by the very fact that it existed. And others drew it. But I, I simply missed it.

19

tuesday, midsummer

THE BARREN PATH, THE STEAMING sun, and the air between the two.

The steam touches his shoulders and brazes his head somewhere just steps from me now. He is just yards away. Somehow, I never let the presence of the thickest black door actually divide him from me. Them from me. It is, rather, a kind of passageway into their world. Though too convicted to break the rules on this side, I find myself too weak to adhere to those on their side. Their rules were plain. Come and go. Breathe in, breathe out. Don't take it in. Inhale just enough to get you through the day, but no deep breaths. Deep breaths force the air down, to the places that do more, that actually process. Then you might absorb the putrid air. You just might become weak, like me. Weak enough to stop smelling the very odors that produce such a putrid scent. Weak enough to come and never really go. Weak enough to breathe it in and absorb.

I breathe in and step one single step through the thickest black door. Greeted by more than I can count, it's as if every guy that Marco has ever met showed up today. I kiss cheeks of strangers, cheeks of acquaintances, and cheeks of our guys. Before I know it, my water bottle is off my shoulder and on to Antonio's. Jorge comes alongside me today, the first to offer me his arm to walk through the pathway. We all filter into the chain link paths, two-by-two, stepping over the sleeping bodies baking in the sun.

"Ju happy?" Jorge asks.

"Sí!" Our simple conversation sounds like two toddlers attempting to communicate, but you would never know it looking at his perfectly tucked in green polo, freshly ironed jeans, shiny boots, and gelled hair. If anyone looks well-educated in this place, it's Jorge.

"You happy, Jorge?" I ask, focusing on him once again.

"Jes." He answers.

"Por qué hay muchas personas aquí hoy?" I piece together six words and hope he knows I'm asking why there are so many people here today.

"Sorpresa." Jorge says a word I've never heard. Well, we hit the lovely language gap once again, but at least I can use my favorite Spanish phrase.

"No entiendo." I don't understand.

For the next minute as our crowd of thirty or forty guys makes its way to the prayer house, Jorge does his best to explain 'sorpresa' to me, but all I get from his gestures is playing peek-a-boo, being scared, and loud claps. I have no idea what's he's trying to convey.

Somehow I lose hold of Jorge in the shuffle to enter the prayer house and get crammed between two large strangers. Guys continue to make their way into the roofless cement building, piling one in front of another until the last man comes in.

Marco is sitting on the folding table, his guitar resting under his elbow until a few guys pull him up and move the table to the middle of the room, front and center. They're clearly in charge today.

I'm starting to breathe in the intrusive smell of these men, who reek of body odor, the kind that seeps into clothing after days of not being washed. Trying to find a bit of fresh air, I move my head back a few inches, but we are so stuffed in this small space that my shoulders are locked in place.

Spanish somethings fill the room, and Marco's head suddenly appears above everybody else's. His laugh fills the air, and I have to push up on my tiptoes to see what's going on.

Sitting on Antonio's shoulders, Marco is propped up in some sort of celebration. Suddenly the room breaks out in worship, "Alabaré, alabaré, alabaré, alabaré a mi señor." Men's voices instantly take a plain, predictable morning and turn it into a loud, praise and worship celebration. Deep, scratchy, high, mostly out-of-tune voices fill the air, undoubtedly reaching those lounging in the pathways.

"Alabaré, Alabaré…" They put a spin on the familiar song, speeding it up, clapping here and there, never in unison. Marco is bounced nonstop, joy filling this place.

Marco's laughter and high-pitched, "Ahhhh" reaches me, and I watch the man who loves them, be loved. After several minutes of bodies clapping, moving, nearly running me over, the voices slow down and end when Antonio finally sets Marco down.

"Ahhhh," Marco tries to recover, wiping the tears from his eyes, tears of love and surprise.

As Pedro steps up, the room quiets and men scoot in toward the middle and sit down, except for those leaning on walls. We stand and listen to Pedro give a speech of some sort. One of the moments I wish Spanish could be learned in an instant.

Pedro's strong voice pauses. As he leads, all heads bow after him, a domino effect. He begins praying, confident, strong in the Lord. I feel goose bumps come over my arms and legs, the presence of God does it to me. As he continues, I begin praying as well.

Lord, touch these men. I pray that if there is one in this place who doesn't have a relationship with You, that they will sense Your presence now and open their hearts to You. God, touch them, speak to them, move the way only You can. Touch these precious souls. God, I hear them, I hear them crying, aching. Oh, God, just touch them.

Paralyzed by the emotion spilling from their souls, I cry too, covering my eyes with my hands to find privacy.

God, You can fill their every need. Lord, please comfort them now. I know Your promises. You tell us You are waiting at the door for us to knock. God, give Pedro the words to lead these men to You. Give him the exact words to show them You are the way to a different life, a more fulfilling life.

I thank You for this time, this place, for using this experience and these men to show me Your boundless love. God, I am so very thankful. Thank You, thank You. For every moment here, I thank You.

Wiping my tears, I open my eyes to a wondrous sight, nineteen, no, twenty. Twenty hands raised in the air, heads bowed. Pedro's voice continues to fill the room and suddenly the voices of the hands echo his every word, souls meeting their Savior.

My eyes capture pictures. Forty-some black heads of hair facing the ground. Dirty knees pressed against a forehead. Shorts and bare feet. An uncovered armpit, arms shot high toward the sky, some heads buried beneath arms. Antonio's mullet and blue wife beater rocking back and forth as he hugs his knees, praying this prayer aloud with the others. Sneakers freshly whitened lead to a man crying aloud, crying through words. Pedro, standing, arms stretched high above his head, calling upon the Lord. Pictures.

Voices stop all at once, leaving just Pedro ending in a strong "Ah, men." Heads lift all over the room, but a few stay firmly fixed to their hands, still praying.

Marco stands up, starts speaking loudly, and men begin shifting, several standing up and moving away from my side. I'm left next to the wall, Jorge just a few feet away from me.

"Maggie, we're splitting the men into groups. We're going to explain what this prayer means. We're going to explain that now that they believe and have confessed their sins, that Christ is their Savior. There is no question. No one can take that away from them. No one. That will be key for these men. They have to understand that what they felt today is forever. Then we're going to talk about learning, reading the Bible, prayer, Bible study, becoming friends with guys here that are believers. How do you feel about leading a group?" Marco asks.

"I'd love to, but I don't want you guys to interpret for me. It'd just be easier coming from you." I say.

"No, no, we have a few who speak English in here. Omar for sure, and I think the bread maker speaks English, too." Marco explains.

"Ok. Sounds good." I agree, ready to serve.

Over the next little while, we form five little groups within the prayer house. I sit with Omar and Cristian, the baker. I explain that this decision is the biggest and best decision they'll ever make. I tell them how important it is to meet with Marco and continue to learn. I get nods from their attentive eyes but not a single question. In fact, Omar is abnormally quiet. I pause again and give them one last chance to ask questions since I see Marco's already done with his group.

"How long ago did you do this, Maggie?" Omar asks.

"Me? Well, about five years ago. I wasn't raised in a Christian family, but I started going to church with some friends, and I eventually felt the undeniable presence of God. I accepted Christ by myself. Alone," I explain, and Omar simply nods his head.

Blessed by immense amounts of discipleship in the years since, I look at his green eyes and wonder where he'll be five years down the road.

Marco's voice brings our group time to a close, and I watch Pedro place a large plastic cup and four flour tortillas on the folding table before sitting next to me. Marco tears the tortillas in half, and tears halves into halves as he tells the story of the night Jesus taught his disciples to break bread and drink wine in remembrance of Him. I can tell we're about to take communion. Communion like I've never seen before.

All eyes look at Marco without exception, these men take in every word. Pedro scoots over and gently touches my arm, "Are you following?"

"Communion, right?" I ask.

"Yeah," he continues to whisper, "he's explaining that we have to go to those we have issues with. If they're here in this room, go to them, make peace. If they're people that aren't here, tell God, and he will hear you. Everyone needs to get their heart right with God before we can pass the bread and water."

I've heard this part of communion time and time again, and I usually spend a moment or two in prayer, praying for forgiveness, mentioning anyone or anything I can think of that needs to be resolved. This is my norm. But never before have I seen anything like this.

As Marco puts down the last pieces of tortillas, he picks up his guitar and sings for us, providing background music as we wait.

Within seconds, men stand and move to people across the room, turn to those next to them, get up and form lines to speak to one another.

I don't know if it's the nature of this place, where men live so close to one another with no distractions, or if it's the simplicity of a trusting, childlike faith, but these men literally go to those they need to speak to, every single one of them. I sit, finding myself watching the newness of this obedience. The longer I watch, the more I'm convinced they are truly doing it right, clearing all issues before coming to God in complete reverence, clearing the sin between them.

It's just a few minutes before I feel a tap on my shoulder, "Maggie, can I talk to you?" Omar's voice is still so much more subdued than normal.

"Of course. Anytime." I say looking at his serious face.

"I'm sorry." His apology catches me off guard.

"We're ok. What's wrong?" I ask.

"I'm sorry. Do I have to say why?" He asks like a child needing guidance.

"No. No, you don't. Whatever's on your mind, I forgive you." I smile at him, assuring him that we are okay. I have no idea what he apologized for, but his honesty is endearing.

As people continue to fill the room with private conversations, the hugs I would expect to end conversations of this sort just don't happen here. The prison world sneaks up every now and then. This is one of those times, the absence of affection. The moments when a head nod substitutes for a pat on the back, for a hug, even for a handshake. These are the times when I'm reminded of where I am.

I stare at the crowded room of men, amazed. Without yet thinking about what's on my heart, I continue to watch them nod and move on to speak to others, never a music-less moment.

Reflecting, I pull my knees to my chest, closing in to examine myself.

Pedro. And Pedro. And Pedro.

Breathing in slowly, I know what I need to do. I stay in my space on the dirt floor until Pedro is free.

Just a minute later, the man who was talking to him stands up, giving me a moment to gently bump into his shoulder.

I start with a simple, "Hey."

"Hey," he answers back.

"Pedro, can we talk for a minute?" I softly ask, my playfulness gone.

"Yeah." He turns to me, so we're face-to-face.

With a sudden sick feeling coming over me, I hesitate. Afraid that what I'm about to say will destroy this fun-loving thing we've got going, I pause, breathe, and push it all aside to say, "I'm afraid I've distracted you. That I've made it difficult for you to stay focused on the Lord. I just want you to know that I love you a ton. A ton. But I'm struggling myself. I don't know what we have, and I don't want to define it because that will change things. I want it to stay exactly like this, but not if it's ungodly. We can't do that. For the sake of all these guys here. For our sake. Look at what you just did! You just led twenty guys to the Lord! Look how God is using you!" I smile, entirely amazed and blessed to watch God use him. "And I want you to keep doing that, Pedro. That's what matters, not me." I say with certainty.

"Whether anything's happened or not, I've wanted it to a thousand times," Pedro says what I never would.

"What now?" I look to him for guidance.

"Let's pray." He reaches for my hand, and I listen to him blow me away once again.

Lord, we are here before You. Forgive me for what I've thought. Forgive us. We want to be Your vessels, usable and pure before you. Cleanse us from all unrighteousness, as Your Word says. God, thank you for Maggie. I thank You for bringing her here to affect so many lives. Help us to walk a straight path and build each other up in Your ways. We don't want to mislead or confuse anyone here. We want to be examples of living a life surrendered to You.

Having this man pray over me draws my soul even closer to his.

We let go of each other's hands, and I focus on Marco, who is just beginning to pass out loose tortillas, hands passing to hands.

Once we all have a piece, Marco briefly prays. The entire room puts pieces of tortillas in their mouths in silence. A few seconds later, Marco prays again, this time taking a quick drink from an orange plastic cup before passing it around the room.

Salvation. It doesn't depend on the fine line.

20

wednesday, nine a.m.

THIS MORNING, I SEE PEDRO the moment the thickest wall opens. Three weeks after seeing him beat so badly, his bruising has faded a lot, his swelling is gone, and his eye is visible once again. Almost back to normal, he is dressed nicely this morning in a plain black V-neck t-shirt tucked in to gray faded jeans and black tennis shoes, freshly cleaned. His hair is still wet, gelled straight back, reaching his shirt.

He leans in quickly to kiss the empty air by my cheek and then walks alongside Marco. I see Omar leaning on the fence and wave in his direction. Not used to having to approach him, I go over to talk.

"Hey, Omar."

"Morning, Maggie. So, Pedro's your guy, huh?" Omar looks at me, still leaning on the fence, no greeting yet.

"No. Not at all. And good morning to you." I say, trying to lighten the mood.

"No, I'm asking you seriously. Do you guys have something going?" Omar's seriousness suddenly makes me wonder what's going on. It sounds like more than a simple question.

"No, Omar, we don't. We are friends. We're close friends, but we're not dating, not at all. We're just working together with Marco." I explain.

"Hope you're not dumb enough to fall for him." Omar says, emphasizing 'dumb enough,' leaving me totally confused.

"Ok. What's that supposed to mean?" I ask, really wanting an answer.

"Just what I said. Don't do that to him." Omar directs. Then he stands up straight and walks to the path, leaving me behind.

I stand next to the opening to the pathway, processing, trying to make sense of what just happened. There are just so many ways to take that. Dumb enough to date a bad guy? Dumb enough to date someone in here? Dumb enough? I can't fight this battle right now.

I think back to prayer in the tent church and remind myself that if Satan can get me discouraged and off-track, then he can interfere with God's plans for the day, and I'm not going to let that happen. Determined, I shake it off and start walking down the pathway.

Omar hurries to catch up with Pedro and Marco, and I can see a new fondness for them, one that wasn't there before yesterday. Omar's hand lands on Marco's shoulder, causing him to turn around and pat his back a few times, making space for Omar to walk with him, leaving Pedro a few steps behind but still a minute ahead of me on the path.

Immediately, men are swarming, aware that I'm not attached to one of the guys this morning. Yellow eyes and a mumbling mouth are the first to approach me, begging for money. Upset that I don't trust him to give him something, I shake my head no, repeatedly saying, "Losiento," apologizing.

Four men with arms full of necklaces, bracelets, carved crosses, and all sorts of handmade items approach me at the same time, one placing a necklace on me, another grabbing my arm, as though measuring me for a bracelet. Speaking Spanish as though I can comprehend their every word, they continuously talk. I stand, surrounded.

Stuck. After just a few steps, I'm stuck with more men approaching.

Even the sleeping guy whose leg I just stepped over is now awake, tugging at my tan capris saying, "Please." Over and over. Too sweet to firmly reject their offers, I find myself smiling, nodding, looking from side to side, wanting to tell them that I'm not interested, but too overwhelmed to. Not able to move past them, I just surrender.

Noticing the constant tug on my pants, I look down and see that the man who sleeps in this same spot every morning, the man whose head is always tucked into his knees, is looking at me. His dimples and inability to grow a real mustache give away his age, and his hand convincingly points for my water. I reach for my water bottle, and the men back up a foot, giving me a little space. Taking my water bottle off my shoulder, I untwist the cap and give the open bottle to the guy who wears a baby face.

As the elderly man starts singing, "Oh, Maaaay – heeeeee," Marco finally turns around and comes back for me. I keep focused on his fatherly face. The minute it takes for him to reach me feels more like an hour with the loud, insistent Spanish requests spinning around me. Still thinking I can understand them, the men continue to say things and hang item after item on me. Now decorated in four necklaces and a wrist full of bracelets, I try to move toward Marco. Not able to tell them that I'm not walking away with their stuff, I give up and wait for him to get to me.

"Basta. Basta. Déjenla, mijos." Marco says softly. And that easily, the men step back. Pulling the necklaces through my curls, I let them remove the bracelets and smile, truly loving every aspect of this place, even this aspect. I feel my water bottle tap my leg and reach down to meet the eyes of the baby-faced man who I'll now forever notice.

"Maggie, what happened to you, Dear?" Marco smiles.

"I was trying to walk alone." I smile back.

"Oh, dear child." He shakes his head then teases, "So, you didn't want to buy a necklace?" His cozy arm wraps around my shoulder, and we walk to the prayer house.

"Marco, can I ask you something?" I turn to the face that's right next to mine.

"Of course, Honey. What is it?" Marco replies.

"You know what? It's nothing." I decide to drop it and maybe bring it up later, although I don't know if I'll ever know what Omar meant.

"Ok, well, let's see who's here today," he says as we approach the prayer house.

I have to pass by Pedro to get into the building, so I slip by, trying not to breathe in his cologne or brush past him, wishing I could be near him without being drawn to his fresh cologne in the morning.

Inside, Maelo, Omar, and Antonio sit on the rugged folding table, surrounded by quite a few of the men from yesterday. Excited to see so many faces, I find a place to sit on the ground next to an empty wall, something I can lean against if we're here awhile.

Hours later, the blares of the bed check break us from a third round of worship, and the men begin to make their way out of the room.

"Omar!" I say his name suddenly and jump up and rush to grab him before he slips out of the prayer house.

As he turns around, I can tell he doesn't want to be bothered, but I've spent most of the morning realizing I need to hear what he has to say.

"Omar, wait up." I touch his shoulder, and he pauses, letting me walk beside him.

"Omar, why did you ask me about Pedro this morning?" I ask with urgency, trying to keep up with his fast pace.

His eyes avoid me. He looks to the right, leaving me alone on his left. "Omar," my hand holds on to his elbow as we walk briskly through the chain link paths, men filing through quickly.

"Maggie, please don't tell me you haven't figured it out." He looks straight ahead, clearly annoyed.

"Figured out what, Omar?" Annoyed myself, I keep pressing.

"Maggie, look at this place." Omar's words mean nothing to me. I have no idea if he's telling me I don't belong or asking me to understand something that I can't fully comprehend because I live on the other side.

"Omar, come on. Be honest. I'm a big girl. Why did you say that?" I need to know if he's jealous or concerned, nosey or cautious. Is he working on my behalf or just working?

"Maggie, meet me here when the check's over. We'll talk. Ok?" His light green eyes meet mine this time, a rarity here, and I know he'll talk.

"Ok. Hey..." My arm grabs on to his just before he goes into his building, "Thank you."

He nods quickly before walking into the crowd of men making their way into his building.

I wait for the blares to end before heading back to the prayer house, knowing I can't do anything while the guards do bed check. Now, with no one around, I step into the chain link path: no bodies to avoid, no offers to reject, no smiles to return, no shoulders rubbing past mine or shouts of my name turning my head. Just me, a dirt path, and chain links all around. The fumes from the landfill permeate my space when no one's near, when they're all far, when it's just open space.

Soft snores greet me as I walk into the prayer house. Marco rests comfortably on the folding table, sombrero over his face, arms crossed perfectly across his chest. Siesta in progress, I take a minute to myself. Looking through my Bible, I turn page after page, searching for blue ink, something written on the left hand side in the margin.

In the midst of fumbling through pages, I find myself praying.

Lord, thank You for another moment, another day with these guys. Lord, I need You to be with Omar and me this afternoon. I pray You give me the words I need to help him understand where my head is and why I'm here. I pray You guide me and give me the right words to speak to him. Give me patience with him and the wisdom to know what his motives are. I pray that this afternoon would be a blessing to You, that lives would continue to be touched. And just give Marco what he needs, Lord. Fill him up while he rests.

Sleepy myself, I use my open Bible as a pillow and lay down on the dirt, quickly falling asleep.

After feeling like I just slept for hours, I open my eyes to Antonio's shoes occupying the dirt in front of me. The sounds of Marco's light snoring still fill the air, and I stretch, wondering if my Bible left an indentation on my cheek.

"Hola, Antonio." I say sleepily, fighting a yawn.

"Hola, necesitas ayuda?" Asking if I need help, Antonio offers me his hand.

"Gracias." I let him pull me up. I smile at his ornery face as he points at Marco, knowing full well he's about to do something.

Laughing, I shake my head no. Antonio keeps suggesting something, nodding in my direction for approval, but this Spanish deficit girl knows Antonio is far too mischievous to agree with anything he might be plotting.

"Shhhh," I whisper, a finger to my mouth.

"Sí, shhh." Antonio softly whispers, content with taking a seat on the dirt.

Pointing to myself, I simply say "Omar" to give Antonio the message that I'm heading over to find him. He nods, and I leave Antonio with Marco in the prayer house.

Constantly moving drips from my forehead to my jeans with a

swipe of my hand, I fight the baking sun. Omar walks in the pathway toward me. Keeping his promise to talk, he nods in my direction.

Just outside the prayer house, we sit on the benches of a weathered picnic table. Across from him, I ask, "Why did you say you hoped I wasn't dumb enough to be with Pedro?"

"Maggie. I'm going to tell you something that you don't want to hear, but you have to promise me something. Ok?" His eyes look at mine this time. Right into mine.

"Ok."

"No, seriously. I'm going to tell you something, and you can't tell Pedro or Marco. No one. Ok?" Omar is serious in a way I haven't seen before.

"I won't." I believe my words as they come out, but I have no idea what he's about to say.

"Maggie, Pedro's got it hard right now."

I listen intently.

"It's you." His green eyes say nothing. I can't get anything but his words. I squint, blinded by the sun, feeling sweat reach my eyelashes.

"The guys that live next to him work in the bakery with me. The day after the guards messed him up, they told us everything about that night."

I wait.

"They were asking him about you the night they beat him." Omar's eyes veer from mine.

He suddenly hesitates.

"Keep talking, Omar. Please." My voice is so quiet that I'm not sure he can hear me.

"I just don't know how to tell you." Omar looks at the table instead of me.

Grabbing his hand to make him look at me again, I simply say,

"Just tell me. Tell me!" Getting angry, I can barely keep my voice under control.

"You want to hear? You can't just take my advice and leave him alone?" Omar asks, anger seeping through his words.

"Leave him alone? This is the first time you've told me to leave him alone. What is going on? You are really upsetting me!" Trying hard not to cry, I look at him, begging.

"They taunted him, Maggie. They asked him how you were, how you felt. They asked him if you were his first white girl, his first time to… to… be with a white girl. They asked if he thought he was better than them. Lots of things. They told him they were going to pass you…"

Omar's eyes fill with tears. I can see into him, half-full of shame, half-full of empathy for Pedro, almost unable to repeat their words. As messed up of a world this is, they always seem to pull for one another in a way I will never know living on the other side. He is full of emotion, pain, surprising pain.

Unable to process, I simply stare at his green eyes, my own tears falling one at a time. Right. Left. Right. Right. Left. Breathing in deeply, my heart drops. It just drops. Straight to the floor. I am the reason? Me? I sit here, trying to process. Trying. I know I have to gather strength. I have to stop these tears, appear fine, and see their faces without showing them a different version of mine.

"Maggie, Maggie." He licks his lips, wipes the sweat from his forehead and says, "I just need you to know. If you back away from him, maybe they'll back off."

Did I really just hear that he was beaten because I'm near him, with him, around him?

That's all I heard.

Instantly, images fly through my mind. His arm on my lower back nearly every time we walk the path, the time I watched him glance to the armor on the wall. Had it already started?

I try hard to focus on Omar.

"But he never did anything, Omar. Never. He never … He never touched me like that. Look at those guys!" I point to the prostitute rubbing up so closely to her man of the day that a little crowd openly gathers to watch.

"Why didn't he tell me? We could've been careful this whole time. Have they done something else? Omar, have they done something else? Is there some reason why you're telling me now and not back then?" I feel myself losing all ability to stay calm, my hands fumbling to wrap up my sweaty hair, tightly pulling every strand back, again and again.

"Maggie." Omar looks down.

"Maybe you can ask Pedro. Maybe he'll tell you." Omar suddenly looks at me, "You know, Maggie, Something happened to me when I prayed and asked Jesus to forgive me. I felt different. I saw Pedro differently, and I don't want something to happen to him. We need him here." His every word overwhelms me.

Burning through my clothes, the sun feels hotter than before, reaching every uncomfortable inch of my skin. Did Omar just say that they need Pedro here? Like he has a reason to think something else might happen to him? What has he heard? Why hasn't someone told Marco, and why is Pedro still hanging around me? Every possible question is birthed within me. So many questions.

"Omar, why do you think he's not safe?" I ask before I realize I probably can't handle any more.

"Maggie. You need to talk to him." With that, Omar stands up and walks back through the chain link toward his building. Leaving me alone to absorb.

Sitting on the picnic table bench, I realize I haven't spent a moment noticing who's come in to the prayer house the last little while, and I have no idea where Pedro is. Desperate to find him, I get up, wipe my eyes off, and regroup.

Glancing in the prayer house, I see a group of guys, Marco's back, but no Pedro. Taking a minute to get to the chain links, I feel sick. If I go to his place, he's with me again. The guards will see us together. If I don't, I don't get to talk to him.

Lost.

Lost, I find myself frozen at the start of the chain links. Disgusted. Just feet from the crowd of men entertained by the prostitute who's nearly mounting her fully clothed companion, I weigh the options. And I know what I have to do.

I can't go. He's worth too much. I can't go. I can't talk to him. I can't see him. I can't even be remotely near him. I can't.

Standing at the opening to the chain links, left going back to Omar, right taking me straight to Pedro, I stand. Motionless. Full of emotion. Torn.

It's torn that brings me to my knees at the entrance to the chain links, unaware of those around me. Instantly burying my head in my lap, I collapse. Collapse perhaps like those I spend moments stepping over each day, collapse like those I think simply need a space in the open rather than inside. Collapse outside on a dirt path smelling in the foul air with every breath, hearing a language I can't yet take in, and not caring about where I am or who's around, only caring about finding a place to let it all spill out.

I collapse on the fine line.

21

thursday morning

As our Bronco outraces little José and the tent-houses fade, my stomach starts filling with knots. The thought of doing something to hurt Pedro in any way kept me up most of the night and almost kept me home this morning. As we get closer to the rocks of the prison parking lot, I look out my window and pray once again this morning.

I have so much hate in me right now, so much hate. I can't think of them daring to touch his precious body, not caring if they break his bones or leave him to die. How dare they touch him! How could they? Lord, I want every single one of them held responsible. You know who they are. You know.

Was it because of me? Did he just sit there and say no, trying to defend himself? Did he hear my name as they hit him again and again? Do all the guys know, and no one said a thing? They didn't even tell Marco. If they had told Marco, we could've helped him. We could've put me with one group and Pedro in another. God, help me know what to do.

Help me, Lord. Show me if I should tell Marco. Please, make it clear. I need some sort of guidance here. I just need You to tell me what to do! I feel so alone. I don't have a person to tell, a phone to call on. I don't have anything, Lord, and this is so beyond me. I've never thought this sort of thing through. I don't know what to do.

Give me strength and wisdom beyond what I can see. God, I know Your Word says if any of you lacks wisdom ask God who gives generously to all. I need Your wisdom now. I'm believing You for that. I don't know where else to turn or what else to do. I'm sitting here begging You to show me what to do. Oh, Lord. I need You today. Take this hate from me. Take this anger from me. Take all of these emotions that are eating me up. Guide me, I pray.

"Maggie?" Marco's hand meets my arm, his gentle voice checking on me. "Are you ready?"

Smiling, I nod and say a simple, "Yeah," but my soul knows otherwise.

After getting checked in and barely searched, I wait for the thickest black door. Standing in line to be let through only a few at a time, I try to see beyond the door each time it opens to let a visitor through. I struggle to see who awaits us on the other side. If Pedro is in his room waiting for me to come to his building this morning, I'll be able to see him alone. We'll be able to talk.

Divided by the wall, we wait.

The guard's harsh hand grabs my wrist as though I'm nothing. I wait for him to let go, to let me go to the only place I want to be.

I step one single step through.

Left to right, I see their early morning faces: Maelo, Antonio, Omar, Jorge, Cristian… Pedro. Trying to hide my disappointment, I greet them one at a time. Antonio first, always first, as his boyish charm boosts him from his spot and straight to the door the second we appear. The others come to us, morning cheek kisses one by one.

Pedro. The face of the man who didn't tell me. The face of the man who was mocked because of me. The face of the man who pretends like nothing is wrong.

His strong cheekbones and defined chin approach my right cheek, the corner of his lips almost meets my skin. A simple "Good morning, Maggie," with a wink.

I'm immediately paranoid. Who saw? Who's watching? Which guard started it all? How many of the guys know? Is everything Omar said true?

Stepping back, I say "Good morning." And I can't stop the smile from coming, the smile that has more attached to it than any other smile.

"Hey, can I talk to you this morning? Just us? Alone?" The words leave my mouth sooner than I expect them to, just moments after walking through the door.

"Yeah, sure. Everything ok?" He asks the question with a quick lift of his chin and a raise of his eyebrows.

I look at his blackest eyes and find myself fighting the desire to comfort myself. How I want to crawl between his strong arms and be held tightly to his defined chest, and rest there indefinitely.

Hesitating and not wanting to lie, I simply say, "I hope so."

My eyes meet his once again, blue on black. The morning sun finds my eyes, causing me to blink repeatedly to keep connected to his. I study his blackest eyes, not willing to let go. Not today.

"Me too," Pedro says, nodding for me to follow the guys who have already started on the path. His hand rests gently on the small of my back, making me nervous, nearly nauseous. I feel his presence behind me, his fingers occasionally meeting my back, letting me know he's right there with me. But this time, it's not reassuring. It's a realization. My shield has been a target all along.

Today, my eyes don't focus on the guys. I trade the grounds for the walls, the prisoners for the guards, the hellos for metal guns. Every guard posed high stands out to me, each one. Although twenty, if not thirty feet higher than us, they are visible. Their motions are without technique, never synchronized, always unplanned. They surround us, some scanning the grounds, others preoccupied with pacing. No real eyes on this place. Only eyes of steel.

After worship and Bible study, Pedro spends a minute talking to Marco, whose repeated head nod signals approval.

"Maggie. Let's spend a little time together. Where do you want to go?" I can't help but be intimidated by the presence of the armor, all around. Should I stage a break up, scream aloud, put on enough of a show to put their assumptions to rest and guarantee his safety?

"Maggie?" Pedro's voice finally reaches me.

"Yeah. Um, where can we go? I don't know where to go." I say, not feeling comfortable behind doors or out in the open.

"How about the table over there?" Pointing out of the prayer house to the picnic table where Omar told me everything yesterday, Pedro waits for my response.

"Ok, that's fine." I agree. I slowly walk the few steps to the table, sick with the thought that everything's about to change.

His stomach caves in when he swings his legs over the bench. Leaning toward me, his elbows rest on the table, his fingers locked. Resisting the urge to comfort him with touch, I let my hands rest on my legs.

"Pedro?" My voice rises, already asking him a question without yet saying a thing.

"Yes," his quick reply and sweet half smile make me even more nervous.

"Pedro, I heard about the night everything happened." I study his face, looking for any indication that he is filling in the blanks, saving me from having to repeat what's haunting me.

"The night everything happened? The night they beat me?" He asks.

"Yeah. I heard." I say quietly.

"I know, Rogelio told me he talked to you and Marco." He says, as though that's what this is about.

"No, Pedro. Yes, I mean Rogelio did tell us what happened, but I heard the rest of it." I look from his mouth to his eyes, waiting for some reaction, some hint of understanding.

"I don't know what you mean, Maggie." He says convincingly.

"Pedro. I know it's my fault." My voice fades a little with each word, almost unable to get them out.

His hand slides from his brow through his hair, the tightening of his face shows he finally realizes why we're sitting here.

"Nothing's your fault." As soon as the strong words come out, he stands up, steps over the bench, and turns to walk away.

I stand up, not ready to let him go.

"Pedro." My voice gets louder, "Pedro."

Stopping at the chain link fence in front of us, his fingers grab it tightly, his head hanging low.

"Pedro," I quietly say, my hand lightly touching his shoulder.

"I need a minute, Maggie." In that moment, I hear Pedro's voice crack.

Without thinking, I gently touch his shoulder and back away, "Ok." I walk away.

Every day I walk away. I take a minute to glance at their faces once more before stepping through the thickest black door. I've learned how to deal with the daily departure, knowing our time away is temporary. But I never walk away on this side. I've never been asked to walk away.

No tears fall. No fight to stop them. I'm so preoccupied with him that I only feel worry, regret. Making my way back to the picnic table, I sit. Setting my foot on the bench, I pull my knee to my chest finding just a bit of false comfort while I wait for him.

His grip on the fence tightens, his arms even more defined. His head looks up now, his shoes shoving dirt to the other side of the fence. Not knowing what he's thinking or what he'll say, I sit. My insecurities take over. Why did I ever come in the first place? Why did I think I should stay? Why did I think God would use a girl who doesn't even speak the language? Do the guards hate me, is that why? Is God's hand in this at all? Has it all just been worthless, pointless? Should I leave?

Pedro turns around and sees me watching him. My chin rests on my knee. I don't move an inch. A trail of tears decorates his dark face.

Stopping a foot in front of me, he puts his hands in the pockets of his faded black jeans, the ones I see a few times a week. I look up at his perfect physique. What is he thinking?

He stands so close but already feels far away. Pedro finally says, "I didn't want you to know."

Lost, I say, "Why? Why wouldn't you think you could tell me? We could have fixed it. I could've stayed home, Pedro. I'd never do anything to hurt you. I don't know why you didn't tell us." With all my focus on him, I turn to the man who has all his focus on me.

"Maggie, why would I tell you? It has nothing to do with you. They would've found a reason." He sits on my side of the bench, battling tears.

"Nothing to do with me? Pedro, it has everything to do with me. Is it true? They asked you about me? They did it because of me, didn't they?" Tears instantly pour out, just saying the words, just imagining it happening makes me hurt.

He moves closer, so I move my knee to make room for him. Side by side, I wait for him to confirm everything Omar said. Moments pass, filling me with fear and regret once again. Maybe I should have left things the way they were.

His arm wraps around my shoulder, right here, out in the open, without a thought about who's watching. I feel his solid arm pull me in close and let my head rest on his chest. We sit. I wait.

Quietly, he says, "Yeah, they did, Maggie. But if it wasn't you, it would've been something else. They don't need a reason for anything. They just wanted to get to me, you know?" Strong, he chooses to comfort me.

Looking up until I find his eyes, I quietly say, "No, I don't know. I don't understand. None of it makes sense to me, Pedro. None of it." He moves his chin, letting it rest on my head, and I keep talking through tears.

"If I had never come, it wouldn't have happened. That's all that's going through my mind. It's my fault. It's all my fault. I just wanted to come help Marco, and I've made it worse for you. You would've been ok." Tears take over before I can finish everything I want to say.

"Come here, Maggie." Already close, I lean in closer, my head buried in his chest. I can feel him kiss the top of my head over and over.

"Pedro, I'm sorry. I'm so, so sorry." I keep saying it over and over.

"Hey," his chin lifts and his arm lets go, "Maggie, stop." His voice is quiet but firm enough to let me know that he's serious. "Listen to me. I won't stop being around you. I'm not going to stop. I don't know if I have a day left with you or a year. I don't know when you'll leave, and I'm not going to let them take a day away from me. I want to be right here, with you, watching you love others. I want to see that smile. You are such a blessing to me. Do you hear that?" His eyes look right into mine, waiting for me. "Maggie," his hand cups my chin, "did you hear me? You are nothing but a blessing to this place, to these men, to me. A blessing, Maggie."

Feeling differently than ever before, I hear this man separate lust from love. I begin to see that this man is truly after God's heart, not mine. I know that Pedro wants God more than me. And I feel a love that's deeper than any I've ever known.

Nodding, I simply say, "I know."

And I do know. I finally know that my time here has touched Pedro in such a way that he has sacrificed his safety to give me more time here with the guys. He's risked himself for another day to see God work, to let me see God's hands in this place, to let me learn and to let others come to know Him. I finally see.

Grabbing his hand in mine, we sit. Nothing more to say. No more tears to fall. Just the hot sun blazing down, the strums of Marco's guitar in the prayer house, a few guards up above, the stench of the landfill all around, men laying here and there, and my soul learning selflessness from this soul.

Here I sit, in the place where there is no fine line, where nothing separates us, where the world turns and spins whether or not we succumb to the rules, to the preconceived ideas of what's right and what's wrong, in the place that allows love and rejects hate. In the place where redemption overcomes evil, where repentance trumps sin, where love stomps out lust.

22

the next wednesday

"GOOD MORNING, ANTONIO!" HIS BOYISH grin greets me this morning, and his painted arm moves my water bottle from my shoulder to his. In my other hand, I carry a new t-shirt, finally remembering to give him an alternative to the blue wife beater that is as much a part of him as his stringy long hair and his tattooed limbs.

"Para tí. Por tí." Not sure of my Spanish, I try to tell him that it's for him.

Pulling off his shirt, he immediately puts on the gray t-shirt and loops his tank around his belt loop. The smell of body odor comes off of him, but it's a smell I've grown so used to it that I actually prefer it over the reeking landfill.

I wonder how Pedro is this morning. Happy and ready to get into our routine, I go ahead before Marco and walk straight to Pedro's building. Seeing him untouched yesterday was such a relief after a few days away.

I can breathe until next Monday.

Passing the candy cart man, I smile, knowing Pedro's just a few feet away.

Approaching the plywood façade, I knock hard on the door three times.

"Hey, Maggie. Hold on. Be out in a minute." Pedro says.

Waiting, I take a quick drink of the lukewarm water in my bottle and lean up against his door, anxious to see the man I've grown to respect. It's something more than his freshly showered body, his recently sprayed cologne, more than the muscles that pop, the eyes that don't end. It's the leader that survived his choices and is making the most of his time here. It's the man that could have sunk into his sorrow but chose to emerge healthier instead. It's the guy who others look to for guidance. It's the guy who has no idea he's amazing.

The plywood moves behind me, startling me for a second, "Hey, good morning." I step back, letting him come out.

"Good morning, Maggie." He leans toward me, letting our cheeks meet. "I've got a surprise for us today."

"You do? What's the occasion?" I ask.

"Wednesday," Pedro smiles, "and that's enough of an occasion for me."

"Ok, well, I'm all for celebrating Wednesdays," I tease.

"Is Marco already in the prayer house?" He asks.

"Yeah, I think so." We walk to the prayer house, and I wonder if this routine is getting old. Filled with insecurity once again, I ask, "Is it easier to meet us there in the mornings? I don't have to come by." I wait.

"Nah, I really like our little morning walks." He answers quickly, not a moment to second-guess his answer. Satisfied, I follow him up the dirt and into the chain link path once again.

After morning worship is done, the crowd returns to their respective buildings to avoid the unbearable sun. Worse than normal, the heat overtakes the prayer house, making everyone uncomfortable. Thinking of the fan in Pedro's room, I hope he invites Marco and me that direction.

I watch them talk for awhile, then they both gather up Marco's guitar, Bible, water, and carry the folding table to the corner before walking toward me.

"Are we heading to your place?" I ask hoping to get out of the heat.

"No, I have something else planned." Filled with a smile of a new kind, Pedro leads us to a small set of buildings I've never approached.

"What are these buildings?" I ask, feeling a little uncertain, never having turned off the path in this direction.

Marco answers, "Conjugal visits are the first two buildings. If you're married, you can pay to use those rooms. The places back here are little shops, tiendas."

What he refers to as "little shops" are much more like miniature shacks at best. There are two white structures, maybe six feet wide, like a little concession booth at hometown football games, only not freshly painted and not stocked with much at all.

The conjugal visit buildings are no bigger than our prayer house, a typical bedroom back home. The lace curtains don't compensate much for the bars they decorate. The mint green paint seems to be the only paint sticking well on this side. I can't imagine coming here to see my husband, to share that space as if it's something sacred. Passing by the rooms feels weird, a place I would've been fine never knowing about.

The concession-like shacks are actual operating stores. Pedro leads us to four white plastic outdoor chairs surrounding a card table. Marco and I take a seat and have a few minutes to chat while Pedro talks to the cook.

"Have you been back here before?" I ask.

"A few times, yes. This is where I first met Jorge. He runs the restaurant right here." Pointing to the small white structure, Marco forgets that I'm an American sitting in a Mexican prison being told that those ten or twelve boards are a restaurant. Has he not seen the look on my face?

"Marco? A restaurant?" I ask, completely baffled.

"Well, Maggie, of course not. But yes, kind of like the taco stands we go to, that kind of restaurant. Good food here, real good food."

With that, I'm suddenly on board because I live for taco stands on the weekends. Somehow in the littlest of spaces comes the yummiest of all tacos: steak, cilantro, lime, green salsa, and white creamy sauce. Within moments of sitting, the smell of grilling hits me and I suddenly crave food that I haven't thought about in months: steak, hamburger, barbeque chicken, kabobs, even just the smell is fulfilling. The moment when you get home and soak in the smell of your neighbor grilling and wish it was yours, and the moment you find out it really is. That's this moment.

Pedro wears the smile he wore this morning, a smile somewhere between happy to give and happy to have. I can't quite explain it, but it's rare in here to see anything but a few smiles: the smile of relief when we walk through the doors, the smile that tries to hide thoughts I never want to know, and the smile that shows they've gotten a hold of God.

"What are we having?" Marco asks. Thankful I don't have to dodge Spanish for awhile, I listen.

"Fajitas. Steak and everything that goes on it." Worried about how Pedro will pay, I find myself absorbing this part of the prison, the walls within the walls. The guys that get to light a grill, cook for others, the trusted few. Pedro must be paying a ton of money to have lunch back here. I can't help but wonder what else this entails.

"So, you said you met Jorge back here, Marco?" Changing the subject, I try to make small talk.

"Yeah, about a year ago, don't you think, Pedro?" Marco fans himself with his sombrero, waving it in my direction for a few seconds, then cooling Pedro, too.

"About that. Yeah."

"Jorge managed a large bank a couple of cities over. He was a great businessman, very wealthy. He has family come every now and then, but he prefers to keep it simple here and spoil his family out there. He only has a few months left, but while in here, he got this place started. He has a friend who cooks and a friend on the outside who brings in food three days a week. That's when it's open or by special request. It's simple business. Profit off of a meal. Mostly trade in here." Marco tells the story in a matter of seconds.

"So, how'd you meet him?" I ask, still missing that detail.

"Pedro and I came back here for his birthday last year. We had been studying for quite awhile at that point, and I wanted to do something special for him, so I set this up. It was a great lunch. Haven't been back to eat since that day!" Marco smiles as he finishes up and looks at me with expectancy.

This will be my first meal here besides tacos and watermelon slushes, my first lunch before noon the entire time I've lived here. A treat among treats.

"What's different today, Pedro? Something's on your mind. You need to talk?" Marco's fatherly instincts sense Pedro's struggle just like they often sense mine.

Hoping Pedro has wisdom, I avoid his eyes just in case they're looking for my approval. I'll leave this entirely up to him. He's the one who is living this every day of his life. For me, it's different. I leave this place. I sleep at ease. He stays here. He sleeps with caution. This is his decision.

Waiting for him to respond in some way, I find myself filled with anxiety. How will Marco react? What will he think? Is he going to trust us through this or question our relationship? Will this change everything? Knowing everything I do about Marco, I have to trust that if Pedro tells him, he'll have wisdom and know what to do.

"A lot, Marco, a lot."

Marco leans in, takes a hold of Pedro's hand, and says, "Mijo, you can tell me."

Something softens Pedro with those words, a wall collapses and brings the whole story with it.

"Some things were said the night they beat me. Pretty harsh things, actually." Our eyes make contact. "Maggie, I'm sorry but I'm going explain part of this in Spanish. It's just easier, and you don't need to know anything more than you already know."

So I sit, not understanding the intense conversation between the two, not knowing if he's repeating what Omar told me or saying something even more graphic. All I know is that Marco is saying very little.

Marco turns toward me, "So you know?" he asks, a bit less fatherly than normal, or perhaps just overly fatherly-like.

"Yeah, Omar told me last Wednesday." I say, ashamed for some reason. Maybe ashamed for not going straight to Marco, but mostly ashamed of even hearing the filth that Pedro had to hear.

"What did he tell you, Maggie? Pedro told me that you know, but he doesn't know what exactly you know." Marco asks but the way he says it is more like a directive than a request.

Feeling pressured, I try to bring myself to say the words that my mind has repeated to itself a thousand times since. "He said they were asking Pedro about me," the words come out as long as I stay focused on Marco, "they asked him if we were together, how I was, how I felt, a bunch of junk, Marco." My eyes fill up, upset saying anything at all, upset wishing Pedro didn't have to associate me with that night at all.

"What else?" Marco asks, his hand grabbing a hold of mine, the three of us now connected by his tight grip.

"Nothing. Really. It was so quick. That morning you rescued me from the necklace guys, remember? Omar just told me he hoped I wasn't dumb enough to fall for Pedro. I talked to him later that day, and he said that was why. The guards did it because of me."

I look at them each for a brief second, trying hard to minimize the whole thing and put it behind us.

"Well, it sounds like we need to talk." Marco lets go of Pedro's hand, his fingers smoothing back his eyebrows.

I stare at Marco, suddenly scared that he isn't receiving this well. Fighting the urge to stand up and walk out of here before hearing what he has to say, I pull my hand from his, landing it on my lap, not sure I can sit through this.

"Maggie, what's wrong?" Sensing that I'm getting upset, Marco tries again. "Maggie, we just need to talk this out. We want the best for everybody, and this is serious."

"Ok." I swallow hard, a gulp interferes with my voice. Chewing the inside of my lip, I wait for whatever the verdict will be.

"Pedro, what do you think? Has anything else happened?" Marco asks.

"Marco, you know how it is here. Really. If it weren't about Maggie, it'd be about something else. It hurt. It hurt a lot. I thought about it for days. Should I stay away from the group? Should I tell you? I was in so much pain physically. I couldn't think. Hearing those things about her tore me up. Rogelio kept telling me they were just trying to get to me, and it's true. So, if I don't come around, they win. If I do come around, they win. They win no matter what."

Pedro's words are directed at Marco, I've become "her" instead of "you." He speaks about me as though I'm not sitting a foot away from him. This surprise lunch has turned into a surprise of another kind, and I find myself frustrated with Marco in every possible way. Why did he have to ask?

"Would you two look at me?" Marco has our immediate attention. "Is there something you need to tell me?" Everything in me hesitates. I know we've never technically crossed a line. If he's really asking if anything has happened between us, I know the direct answer is no. But what if this one question includes all the in-betweens? Is it the all-encompassing: Do you like each other? Do you feel something? Do you love her? Is there a reason the guards think you're together? Is there something you've hidden? To those questions, I don't think I can lie to the man who has brought me here with him every day, who has opened his home to me, and made me his family. To those questions, I only know that the moments I have known this man have been more meaningful than any other. Though innocent of sex, I was guilty of some undefined measure of love.

Pedro looks at Marco and says with certainty, "No, we're not doing anything, Marco." His words are true. We are not doing anything.

"Ok, that's what I thought. You know, Maggie, there is evil, such evil. I think I shelter you from that. We come here every day, and I've shown you wonderful guys with soft hearts, but we can never forget that Satan is always at work. Always. He will do anything he can to destroy God's people from making an impact. Look what just happened! Pedro led these guys to the Lord. Well, not before Satan tried to take him out. We keep our faith in God strong. He is mightier than Satan, so much mightier. Let's not lose hold of that. It seems like the guards are the enemy, but it's their souls that have to be transformed before their actions can change. We have to pray for their souls to soften, Maggie. They're not the enemy. You know what they are? They're deceived. Victims of Satan, deceived. We were all there once, weren't we?" His fatherly eyes come back and wink at me, grabbing my hand in his once again. "We were all there." His eyes close, and he silently prays, still squeezing my hand tightly.

My eyes find Pedro's. Smiling at me, he mouths, "You ok?" I nod. I am. I am perfectly ok and entirely relieved. Feeling so much better knowing it is out in the open, I am completely fine.

A guy in a white apron approaches us, three plates in hand. The smell of our grilled steak is the single greatest smell I've known. Breathing it in slowly, I smile, barely able to wait for tortillas, limes, white sauce, salsa, and every little bowl to decorate the table. Cut into bite size pieces, my plate is full of steak and two enchiladas with reddish brown sauce. Afraid I won't be able to stomach it all after weeks of two small meals a day, I stare and decide all of the food is going down, whether it fits or not.

Marco opens his eyes and says a prayer aloud to bless the food. Every bite is perfect. We sit, not addressing the issue again until the very end.

"Are you two okay? Maggie? Pedro? Anything you need from me?" Marco checks on us once again before we get up.

"I'm fine. I just want Pedro to be okay. He's the one who has to deal with it." I neglect to mention the million other thoughts I have.

"I'm okay. Marco, you said it perfectly. It's not them. I have to somehow start to pray for them. I just have to. If someone wasn't praying for me, I never would've changed my life." Pedro puts it so simply.

The fine line that doesn't want you to forgive, that doesn't see the good, that only knows the act, not the potential. The fine line that Pedro has buried after being on the other side.

23

thursday morning

THE SUN WAKES ME, BUT it never wakes me. Marco wakes me. Sitting up, I reach for my glasses, roll off my floor mattress and make my way into the living room. Drinking coffee as though it's Sunday morning, Marco looks up from his devotional, all dressed and ready to go. No music to wake us, nothing.

"Marco, what time is it? You didn't wake me for prayer." I move to the sink and hurriedly put my contacts in, an inch from the mirror. Struggling to wash my face and figure out what to put on, I wait for Marco to answer me. Instead I turn to find him and Maria sitting at the table, both quiet.

"Ven, Maggie. Ven." Maria's words are gentle, but I don't like the mood in here. I don't like it at all. Lost, I sit in my pajama shorts and tank top in a blank stare. What's going on? Is something wrong? Maybe we're taking a trip to the States, maybe something came up last night.

"Maggie, Maria and I talked last night. We both think it's best for you to stay home from the prison for awhile. Maria can use some help around the house, and she would love to spend time with you. There are..."

I think he keeps talking, but all I hear is stay home from the prison for awhile, and then I disappear. I disappear. No! No! No! I won't! I can't! No, not without telling them. Not without knowing beforehand. No, it's not right. It's not fair. His voice keeps going, as though I'm listening, and all I can do is think of everything I need to say but can't now. No, no, just one more day. Just. One. More. Day.

Filled with tears, not just one or two, but an entire flood drowning my skin, I get up and grab the towel I just washed my face in. Bawling, I sit, bawling aloud. "No. No, Marco, please!" I quietly cry. "Just today. Can I just go today, say goodbye, please…" I cry and shake and notice the clock for the first time. 9:05. "They're already waiting. It's not fair. Marco, please!" I cry. Without a moment to process or a chance to see it coming, I react. React instantly and instinctively, raw emotion.

The next minutes are silent. They are talking, but I don't hear them. I wipe my face and beg, again and again. Beg to see them one more time. Beg to not be the person that they thought I would be, disappearing with no notice. Beg to leave with integrity, decency.

But Marco gets up and picks up his guitar, plants a kiss on my forehead, sending my cries into a loud mumbling, and he goes. He leaves. He drives to the place I belong. He gets in the Bronco, and I know that by the time the clock says 9:40, he'll be there with them. Without me.

"No, Maria! Please? What happened?" I try to calm down so I can hear what she has to say then I feel the soft touch of Rosie's hands on my shoulders.

"What's the matter?" She hugs me from behind, her petite arms holding me tight.

"Your dad doesn't want me to go. I just want to go…" The words escape through my tears.

"Shhhh. It's okay. It's okay. We'll find out why, ok. Maybe it's just today. Hold on, okay? We'll figure it out."

Our late night giggles and her tales of boys have gotten us close, but Rosie only knows about Pedro's beating. Nothing more.

That morning, we go into Rosie's room, Maria following us. We sit on the bed and I hear what I already know in my heart. They talked last night, and after much thought, decided it would be best to keep me away. Best for me. Best for Pedro. Best for all of them. I hear it all, I really do. Each word makes sense. I even thought about it the day after Omar told me, but nothing eases the pain, the ache to be there. Nothing. Eases. The. Ache.

The fine line tells you what you fear most, it feeds your doubts, it creates pain. The fine line keeps you safe, or so it makes you believe.

24

two weeks later

IT BECOMES A BLUR IN my mind at times. How it can is so frustrating. I can hardly feel it as much as I try. I want the harshness. I want the walls to stand before me with all their cold stares. The forsaken cells that aren't so forsaken. The dirtiness of the guards' stares. I've forgotten so much: how the water tasted so fresh after my saliva had been used to quench my thirst for hours, how the sun beat down differently on that side, how my stomach craved watermelon and just how soothing it tasted in there. I'm forgetting. The smell that I hated I now long to inhale. The sounds of men's voices singing hallelujahs in the midst of the morning, the faces, their faces. I'm forgetting their faces. I said I would never forget. I swore I would never forget. And I want it all before me. I want to breathe that air. The air that aches to be refined. I want to watch them sing. The singing that goes beyond the lyrics. I want to see their faces. Faces that are disappearing. All I can do is dream. Dream of them and me.

And blame the fine line.

25

a saturday

TWENTY-THREE DAYS WITHOUT SEEING THEM. Twenty-three days of watching Marco go and staying behind. Although hours of talks with Maria are okay, nothing fully distracts me these days. From nine until five my mind is there with them, walking the grounds, fighting the sun, singing the songs, flipping pages in my Bible, keeping them on the right verse, meeting new faces, embracing the old ones. Every day, it's the same. My heart is there, leaving me unequipped to fully absorb much here.

Still towel drying my long curls, I hear words I've been dying to hear, "Maggie, you can come to the prison with me today." I nearly fall forward, afraid I made it all up.

"Really? Oh, Maria!" My eyes fill with tears, my legs jump up to get ready.

Placing her warm hands on my cheeks, she says, "Yes, Maggie. To the women, dear. We will go to the women's side. I haven't gone in several months, but I know they'll be happy to have company."

My heart sinks. Just seconds after returning, it falls hard. How can I be that close and not see them?

"Maria, I don't know if I can go and not see them." I stare into her eyes, pleading for a moment with them. I see the love in her eyes. She quickly kisses my forehead and tells me to get ready.

I don't know if I'll see them, but if I do, it will be the last time. Staring at my clothes, I don't know what to wear. Everything's clean. Long days in a quiet house meant tons of washing on the back porch, hanging over a line to dry, washing, hanging, folding. Hours of swinging on the simple hammock attached to the iron bars that emerge from the cement porch walls, waiting, hoping, wondering. Hours leading me to this moment.

I stand, following the routine like always: lift the shirt, turn up the wired cup of my bra, pull out my pockets, turn around. But this is the first time my stomach jerks in and out, my lips responding to the quiver in my chin, my throat gulping. My mouth tries to stay shut, but moans from my soul cannot be contained.

It's in this moment that the guard in the closet looks toward my face. I can feel her trying to make eye contact. Not today. The guard who never learned my name sees the ache that is smeared so carelessly on me now. I bend over and grab my chest with my fists, looking at the floor, ashamed.

I wait for a shove out the door into the waiting area where Maria will reconsider her kindness and lead me out the door, down the gravel road, and back home.

"Pobrecita. Levántate." Stand up? A peaceful, "Stand up?" She meets my eyes with something so foreign here, empathy.

I have no idea what she said to me in those next few minutes. I don't know if she spilled out a story of loss and love or if she told me to get my act together and see a psychiatrist. But I do know that I walked out of the closet with dry eyes. Only a few wet marks told the secret, the one my Maria already knew.

The path never looks this dry. The only patch of grass is half buried in dirt. Even the grass looks weak today. The walk is long. Slow. I pause too many times. Straight before me is the thickest black door. Just a quick turn to the left lies the door that leads to the women's side.

We fall back from the first group of visitors to enter and join the second. I keep my eyes down. I can't bear to look up. I can't stand the thought of spending my day with women that I've never met when my men are a wall away.

Lord, please!

As our group approaches both doors, a few visitors step to the left, others continue straight ahead to the men's side. I watch the bottom of Maria's long colorful skirt sway after she steps. Covered in red and orange flowers, it moves ahead, oblivious. It's our turn. The guard to the left or the guard straight ahead?

I glance down at the inkblot on the inside of my left arm and feel for the number in my back left pocket.

Maria turns back and waits for my eyes to meet hers. I fight the blinding sun and try to smile a grateful smile though my heart is pounding with fear that my last chance will pass me by with a shift to the left. Then, my Maria points straight ahead.

I breathe in deeply.

Thank You.

That quickly, I am about to take one single step through. Here is my chance. All I have to do is see the line. I see where the dirt path meets the black metal doorframe. I follow the foot of black metal until it touches another dirt path.

Shoes are before me, some laced, others not. None are Pedro's.

"Which way, Maggie?" Maria gently touches my hand.

It's in this moment that I realize Maria has never seen me here. She has only seen the Maggie on the other side of the wall. Will she understand? Does she see them? Like we see them? Marco says only a few can do it. Is she one?

Reconnecting, I respond, "Where? Pedro's?"

A simple nod lets me know that she is showering me with grace, allowing me a goodbye.

"To the left, we just follow this path all the way to the left. His is the second building, the furthest one from us."

The words come out, barely come out. This time my eyes don't meet theirs. As hard as I want to smile as my old man greets me with the same old song, I don't. My fingers drag along the chain links, and Maria takes care of all offers to buy the latest wooden key chain. The only way I can do this is to focus on the ground beneath.

I *can't* see them.

"Maggie!" Sweet Maelo grabs my arm. The touch of his young hand upon my tanned skin loosens all my nerves and brings me home again.

"Maelo, how are you?" I cup his flawless face in my left hand before kissing his right cheek.

"Bien, estás vistando a Pedro?" Maelo asks.

"Sí." Yes, I'm visiting him.

I can see that Maria is taken a bit off course by my greeting here in this place. The line hit her the moment the thickest black door opened. It tells her a kiss upon the cheek is not ok here. I can see her eyes change a bit, the mother within emerging to protect my poor decision-making. I'm doing exactly what I've always done here, what Marco always sees, what Marco models.

As soon as we leave Maelo, Maria turns to me, "Maggie, some guy is going to see ju planting kisses on cheeks. Ju don't want that. That's not jur purpose here." Maria firmly holds my hand and stops walking, looking straight into my eyes.

"Not my purpose? What's my purpose, Maria?" My tears are ready to explode, finally ready to cry on their behalf, to get it all out, to challenge it all.

My tears want to scream.

My mind wants to reason.

My heart wants his.

"To minister, dear. To help Marco. Maggie, look at me." Her hand meets my chin. "This is a prison. Ju don't know who these men are. Ju probably believe their lies They have a way to manipulate. Now, ju say jur goodbyes. Ju kiss a cheek and think nothing. This is jur friend. But he sees ju a beautiful girl and wants anything. Ju kiss him, he take. Ju hug him, he take. He sees ju body, not ju soul, Maggie."

The line.

"Maria," My voice is so quiet I wonder if she can even hear me as I stare at the red polish freshly painted on my sandaled foot. She doesn't understand. I guess my purpose here is not reflection of who Christ is and how he loves the unlovable. At least we all agree on that, the unlovable. So would Jesus teach at an arm's length, ever-cautious, ever-hesitant, waiting for the monster to attack? Or would he breathe in deeply, again and again? Forgiveness preceding judgment and judgment overthrown by mercy. "I know, Maria, I do."

That's the truth. I do know. I do know some see me that way, but not my boys. Others perhaps, maybe all the others. But what are the chances that the vultures in this place are the majority, yet I haven't met a single one? Some would say the odds are great. That if 'danger' were plastered on their foreheads, I would still miss it.

There is no use arguing with the line.

The usual trail of men decorates the length of the cement building. Some keep to themselves. Others stare. He is somewhere close, within these walls, just steps away. How many more times will I stand so close?

Absorb? My fingers shake for the first time ever. It's a physical reaction that I know others experience but never me. Nothing has ever had the power to make my hands tremble. Will Maria notice? Somewhere beneath her sweetest smile and concise agenda for the day, I know she feels my pain. There must have been a conversation with Marco in the night, whispered far from my ears. She knows my need. Somewhere the girl within her feels the girl within me. I know she only brought me with his approval.

Today, I won't look. Today, I won't see. Today will be the day that I close it all off and say a painless goodbye to the nobodies who reside here. Today, I have to.

Knocking on his plywood door with visibly shaking hands, I wait to hear the one voice I've ached to hear every single day. No letters sent home with Marco, no messages from him, not even a hello. Nothing.

Rogelio's voice answers with a quick, "Un momento." A moment, I barely have. I look at Maria, wondering just how long she'll give me before we head to the other side.

The door opens, and I still don't know if he's inside. "Hola, Rogelio. Esta Pedro?" Asking if he's home, I feel sick at the thought of looking at him just one more time. Will we ever walk these paths again, feel the closeness of each other's company? Will I leave with nothing but a goodbye?

"No." Motioning for us to go inside, Rogelio heads off to find Pedro. I look to Maria before stepping in. She smiles and I find myself in this place, in Pedro's room on a Saturday in August.

Will Rogelio tell him I'm here? Or will he just tell him someone is here?

Within minutes, Pedro's familiar voice meets his neighbor's voice. Would he have stopped to chat if he knew I was here? Would he let anyone interfere with our time together? Feeling nervous, I close my eyes and breathe. Almost time.

His hand meets the plywood. Caked in dirt, it pushes the door open, hands I would've given anything to touch for weeks. He steps in and sees me, stopping in immediate shock. "Maggie."

His eyes search for something to wipe off his hands, but I grab them as they are, and hug him tightly, placing a quick kiss on his cheek. Still in disbelief, he stands, barely moving. Finally breathing in, he says, "Maria, it's good to see you." Pedro smiles right at her.

"Just a minute," He turns from us and begins dampening a towel in the shower. Maria breaks the silence by making small talk with him. All washed, he properly greets her, inviting us to take a seat on the bed. Surprisingly, my Maria simply says, "Maggie, I will be outside the building. Ten minutes, ok?"

"Thank you." Her sweet cheek meets mine along with a quick squeeze of my hand.

Still in shock, he stands before me, quiet. The plywood door comes to a quick close, and I whisper, "Pedro, what did Marco tell you? Because I didn't know. I just woke up the next day, and he left without me." I look at him, desperate for him to understand that I miss him that I want to be here, that it wasn't my choice.

Stepping toward me, he draws me in close, his fingers resting on my hair, "I know. I know."

"Pedro, I miss you." My voice already breaks, and the tears I've held back come pouring out, "I've missed you, I've missed this place. I didn't want to leave."

Somewhere between comforting me by holding my head to his chest and repeating, "I know, I know," we find ourselves vulnerable in each other's arms.

His strong arms hold me, letting me know he understands, letting me know that my worries all these days weren't founded, letting me know that the connection we have goes far beyond my doubts.

Not wanting this to end, I look at the man I may never see again, and feel his skin warm mine. I let him put his fingers through my hair, breath in the smell of my perfumed neck, have a moment in the world of a woman, a world so far from here.

Knowing we have no time, my tears reach his cheeks. Wiping them from my eyes, he places soft kisses on every inch of my face, ever so softly. I gently touch the hands that hold my face.

"It's almost time, Maggie. Maria's waiting." He says. Wishing I had said something meaningful, I stand, his hands in mine.

"I know." How do I say goodbye?

I simply whisper, "I don't know how to say goodbye, Pedro." My blue eyes meet the black eyes that I fell into so many weeks ago, and I wonder how I will ever find my way out of them.

Our lips nearly touching as we speak, he simply says, "You taught me how to love, Maggie."

And I look at the man who taught me so much more. Speechless. No words can explain my heart. No words.

A hard knocks sends us back to the world we must embrace. "Maggie, are ju ready?" Maria asks the only question I am prepared to answer with certainty. "No, but I'm coming." And just like that, we let go.

My hand opens the plywood door, Pedro a step behind, and I pause to wipe my eyes one last time. Eyes that see a soul.

I know that I will have to be strong for the hours before the stamp on my arm expires. I will have to meet women, smile, and pretend to be present.

I will have to go on without him right here and face the indefiniteness of ever seeing him again.

Or I will step one single step back through and finally see the fine line. The line that will erase these eyes and make the days more bearable, make the nights more restful. The line that will tell me he is nothing. The line that will teach me to call them nobodies and call myself a somebody. The line that will take these feelings and make them weaker, take this skin and make it thicker, take this life and make it simpler. The fine line.

26

later that weekend

SATURDAY NIGHT WAS HARD, A night of toying, tossing, turning, and finally praying in an attempt to make sense of it all. A night of asking God to give me peace, to take away the confusion, to give Pedro what he needs.

Sunday morning at the tent church was even harder. The sounds of hundreds of voices calling out their requests to God simultaneously, all around me. Too fragile, I couldn't feel the closeness I once felt. I couldn't tune in to worship either. I only stood, the warmth of Maria's hand holding mine… her hand holding mine. Every moment was a reminder. Her hand, not his. Worship here, not there. Marco listening, not leading. Voices feminine, not male. Surrounded by open-air, not closed cement walls. Freely moving bodies, no guards monitoring. A folding chair, not a dirt seat. Church here, not there. Me here, not there.

I tried to keep tears from sliding out the entire afternoon Sunday. Finding myself laying in the stringy hammock that hung from the cement wall on the back porch, I waited for something other than Diego's cartoons to happen in the few rooms we called home. Something to focus on, to think about, to distract me. But nothing did, nothing other than a long nap.

Sunday night I found myself snacking on popcorn and coloring with Diego when Marco called me over to the dining table. We hadn't spent much time talking since I had been staying home. Hearing about his days at the prison was too much for me. So, hearing him say my name threw me off. I took a seat in a rolling chair, next to the man whose days I envied.

"Maggie. I miss you." Marco said.

My eyes instantly filled with tears that couldn't be restrained. I missed him too. In so many ways.

He placed a kiss on my forehead, resting there for a moment before taking each of my hands in his, "Maggie. The guys miss you, too. I want Pedro to be safe. I didn't know what to do. But I believe that God has you here for a reason."

I didn't know if Maria encouraged it or if God Himself prompted Marco. I only knew that my Saturday August goodbye was just a prelude to another week at the prison.

A prelude to the fine line.

27

tuesday nine a.m.

TODAY. NO LAST GOODBYES. NO reasons why. No ache walking out the door.

The thickest black door slowly opens, guided by the hand of a glassy-eyed guard, one who never says hello or goodbye, sure or thanks. One who coldly glances at my ink stamp and moves the bar to free the door to open.

Glancing up, I smile at the perfectly white puffy clouds, the light blue sky, and the ever-shining sun. Waiting for Marco to step through, I feel for my number in my back left jean pocket. Pulling my white tank down, I straighten my layered turquoise top and flatten my lips together, smoothing my just applied lip-gloss.

There isn't a moment of doubt or hesitation, nothing but joy this morning. After weeks without morning prayer or this door to step through, I'm thankful for another day. Today, I can see all of their faces. I can look at each one of them with intensity, seeing the lives that live on the other side. We can visit. We can worship. We can reconnect.

One single step through.

No shoes. No Antonio. No guys to grab our belongings. No one to greet us. No one to meet us.

"Where is everybody?" I ask, wondering if something changed since I last came.

"I don't know. Let's head to the prayer house and see."

The chain link pathways are full like always. The baby-faced kid still sits in his spot, his sunken head doesn't see mine. Some sit, others sleep, a few stare at us as we walk by. I soak in the atmosphere, the place I left so suddenly. Nothing has changed, but I can taste it now. I can smell the stench of the landfill, stronger than I remember. I can hear the sounds of morning birds, a few voices here and then, mostly a quiet morning. I embrace this side of the wall. Breathing in. Breathing in. Just like before. And I feel time expand with each step we take, a trip to another time zone where moments turn to minutes and hours turn to days.

"Maggie, how are you feeling?" Marco winks in my direction, my arm linked through his.

"I feel good. It's so good to be back! Marco, thank you. I know you didn't have to." I squeeze his arm as we approach the prayer house.

Anxious to see them, I peek my head in first.

Nobody.

"Let's swing by Antonio's first. It will be easy to pick up all the guys from the north and then head back to grab Pedro." Marco suggests.

"Sounds good." Still thrown off a little by their absence, I check to make sure everything else is the same. Guards scattered throughout the grounds, people everywhere.

"What do you think is going on?" I ask, a little disappointed to have to wait to see them.

"Well, I'm not sure, but I've had a few days like this. Antonio's almost always here, but sometimes if he's not, I have to go recruit. You never can plan your day. You know that, Maggie."

He's right. There hasn't been a single day in this place where we stuck to a plan. A song will spark a request, a request will bring up a question, a question will lead to a study we never knew was coming. The joy of this side of the wall. Meeting needs as they come.

The watermelon cart is coming into view, the sweet elderly woman unpacking her cooler in their regular spot. Another day together, though apart. The basketball court is empty this morning, a bit unusual for the morning hours. Men are perched in their cages, one after another, arms hanging out their windows to feel the morning breeze. Men come toward the chain links, moving past us to find something or someone to bring meaning to their day. But no one flocks to us this morning. Not a soul.

The entrance to Antonio's building is blocked by men hanging around. Marco makes his way, a firm grip on my hand, and pulls me through the crowd. There's never been a crowd, not a crowd with this feel, and for the first time ever, I feel like something's wrong.

We turn to the left, just a few more cells until Antonio's. The bars reveal the inside of each cell, a guy laying on his bunk in the first, a man looking out his window in the second, and no one anywhere in the third. No Antonio.

"Well, let's check on Jorge." Marco says, unphased.

Following him to the other side of the building, something seems to be drawing the men out of their cells. They talk in clumps, no selling items or lounging about. They congregate.

"Jorge!" Marco calls for him and shakes the bars of his cell in case he's in the bathroom, but no one answers.

"Well, Mags, let's head back to the prayer house. They know where to find us." He says it so simply, as though it's just another normal day, but something stirs within me, an unsettling. A major unsettling.

Managing to filter through the guys and exit the building, we walk to the prayer house in silence. Silence accompanied by this world I love.

Taking in the space again, a tan shoulder covered in a sun tattoo passes by mine, and a kid runs to the south side, quickly grabbed by a guard, the only time I've actually seen a guard touch someone in here. Bright buildings hide the mini-restaurants, chain link after chain link after chain link bring us to the prayer house. A cold, empty prayer house.

Sensing Marco's uneasiness, I bring myself to smile and lighten the mood, "Well, this isn't the Tuesday I expected!"

Smiling, he reaches for my hand, "Maggie, let's pray. Father, we lift these men to you. Lord, we ask you to come into this place, to cover it with Your presence. Father, may Your mighty hand be felt here…" A pause much too long to be a simple pause for words. A pause leaving me wondering what to do. Do I finish for him? Do I wait? Is it my turn to pray? Is Marco okay?

Just as I open my mouth to begin, his voice fills the room once again, "Mighty, powerful, Comforter, Counselor, Prince of Peace, Forgiver, Redeemer, Name above all names, worthy of all praise, the Highest, we lift You up, we stop at the sound of Your Name, we bow at Your creation, we lift our eyes to You, we need Your direction. Rey de Reyes y Señor de Señores, en el nombre de Cristo Jesús. En el nombre de Cristo Jesús, en el nombre de su Hijo, oh Gloria a Dios. Be glorified in this place. Be glorified. Above all else, we will glorify Your name."

Marco's words stop, but as my eyes open, I find him still praying, lips moving, head bowed, a prayer for God alone. Lost, I simply wait for direction, expecting Marco to hear clearly from the Lord. Maybe this Tuesday wasn't meant to be after all, but how could they just stop meeting? Marco didn't say anything. Is he keeping something from me? Does he know what's going on and he just hasn't said anything? Where are they?

My mind continues its stream of possibilities until I see Marco's eyes meet mine. "Maggie, you are precious. Do you know that?" My eyes meet the man I love so dearly with a look of thankfulness. "You are precious. I'm so glad to have you here with me again. They are going to be so excited to see you. So excited. Don't doubt that, Dear. If they knew you were coming, they would have been waiting. You know that, right?" And I nod at this precious man who is more concerned about me than them.

"They must be at Pedro's. There's not much other than the south side. Let's go on over." Careful not to ask to go to Pedro's first thing this morning, I'm relieved that Marco makes the suggestion.

Armed with our Bibles, his guitar, and water for the day, we hit the path again. The usual presence of the woman in her thigh-hugging jeans stands in our way, still deciding which man will ease her insecurities this day. Passing by her crowd of options, we walk to the right, nearly alone in this last pathway before reaching the south side.

The open land before us is barren, as usual. But unlike every other day, Pedro's building isn't lined with men of every sort. No wall of men forms a welcoming, no eyes to look back at us. Not. A. One.

"Where is everybody?" I keep my arm linked to Marco's even though we walk an open field alone. I feel safer, safer arm-in-arm. And something within me needs to feel safe right now. The norms on this side have formed a familiarity that's gone this morning. A familiarity that left the moment the thickest black wall opened to no one at all. The familiarity that brings a comfort, a predictability that says a crowd won't block the entrance to Antonio's building and the wall of Pedro's building will be lined. Every day. No matter what.

The comforting familiarity. Gone.

Looking up, I glance one time at the guards standing above, stationed as usual, stationed without a change. A hint of familiarity, the armor actually brings me comfort this morning.

As we approach the building, a flood of voices nearly stops us from entering, though their faces are far away. We walk down the cold cement hall to the place where the candy cart usually awaits us. But this morning, I can't see the cart. I can't see the cell in front of me. There is no open area dividing Pedro's cell from the cells across from it. Shades of brown fill the space. Men everywhere. No space for Marco to pull me through this crowd. No view of Pedro's plywood door. This morning I stand and stare at men in a huge huddle of sorts. A huge huddle.

Unable to understand their words, I see this side's unthinkable, arms around shoulders, men embracing men, and men's hands resting on men's shoulders. The loud yells and simultaneous conversations all bring chaotic, unorganized noise to my ears, leaving me confused. My Marco simply grabs my hand tight and says, "You wait here, Maggie." Pulling a man I saw on communion day next to me, he replaces his own hand with this stranger's and leaves me.

As Marco tugs on shirts, trying to force his way through, I watch eye after eye catch a glimpse of Marco and back up in respect, spreading apart, making a walkway to the middle of their huddle.

Following after Marco, I clench the hand of my stranger and walk with reservation, not knowing if I will be afforded the same allowance to enter this space. But faces meet mine and equally part.

Before me a good ten feet, I see men on knees, others standing, some laying down, our men. Why our men? My eyes fill with tears, not the tears that know why. Tears that fall for someone else's pain, someone else's cries. Tears that emerge in that moment before the soul learns the cause. Tears sparked by the soul's prompting rather than a man's words.

These tears don't need man's words. No, not these tears. These tears only need eyes to see. To see that gray t-shirt tremble and hear loud Spanish somethings screamed from his mouth. To see Omar's green eyes meet mine and shake his head no, just shake no. To see a pile of men in a circle on the floor, sealed off by a hundred more. To see my Marco grab black heads of hair into his chest, comforting our guys.

As though panicking, Marco's body quickly turns toward me, "Maggie! Maggie…" As he steps toward me, I know that he wants to take me away, take me from this place, but there is a reason why I am here this morning. After weeks of being home, this day is not a mistake. As I breathe in slowly, I feel a need to step forward, to insist, to be a part of this day.

"Maggie, please." He pleas with me.

"Marco, I need to go." My words come out simply, matter-of-factly. I have to see.

And with that, Marco steps aside and allows me to step closer. Somewhere within he knows that in the same way he feels their ache, knows their pain, and loves them despite their sins, that I, too, need to experience this for myself. I, too.

But nothing, no words prepare my soul for the impact or my eyes for the horror. For as Jorge shifts his body, and Antonio covers the face of the man who is on the ground, I know. My soul knows.

It's Pedro. The one who knows the touch of my hand and the taste of my tears. The one who quiets me and listens when I don't have a thing to say. The one who knows my heart and knows my love.

It was Pedro.

On the floor.

Lifeless.

I don't move. I don't say a word. I don't cry. I don't scream. I don't even feel. I simply stare. And as I stare, each dear friend of mine touches another, a touch to give me a moment now, now that they have had theirs.

Staring, never once taking my eyes from his hands, the hands I will never know well enough, I stay locked on the fingertips that just, just brushed through my hair. Antonio finally moves, leaving his face for me to see. He is fully exposed, all of us gathered around, and it's my turn. It's my turn.

I see the dirt floor and want to be there, so my knees meet the rough ground next to his stomach. I pick up the hand that shouldn't feel cold. I touch the fingers that aren't wrapping around mine, and hold them anyway, rub them to warm them, place them next to my neck, holding them close, close, close… and look at the face that isn't the face that knows mine.

This face is split on the cheek, blood-soaked, not his. It's not his. My fingers touch his cheek. My fingers try to clean it. But the blood just smears. It just smears into his hairline. It can't be like this. I take my shirt off, exposed in my white tank, a shirt inappropriate for this place. My white tank. Inappropriate for this place of murder.

Staring at his closed eyes, I feel for the strap of my water bottle and hold it, carefully twist the cap off, and pour it over my turquoise top. Squeezing the excess water, I carefully begin cleaning the smears of blood from this face. Wipe. Move to a clean piece of cloth. Wipe. Move to a clean piece of cloth. Wipe. Gently dab the wound, but it's too big, the gap's too big. He's going to need stitches. "Marco, he's going to need stitches." My eyes look up, finding Marco standing over me. "Marco, stitches. We need stitches. They'll see him today. They have to see him today." Marco's sombrero is motionless. He's not getting help. We need help.

"Maggie, Maggie." Marco's quiet words keeping coming. He keeps saying my name. I hear him say my name, but I'm not moving. I'm not leaving him. I'm staying here. "Maggie, he's gone. He's gone, Maggie." I know. I know he's gone. He is not here. Not my Pedro.

I feel a hand on my back, but I don't turn, I stay here, focused on him, seeing him, brushing his hair back into place. I can't get it right. His hair's not right. It's not right.

Picking up my wet shirt again, I follow the blood trail down his neck, wiping each spot, wiping, wiping it clean. Opening his button, I keep wiping. The entire left side of his shirt is soaked in blood. Second button, more wiping, more wiping. Third button. Wiping the cut.

Stabbed. Wiping, I pour my water right on his chest, my shirt too soaked to help anymore. My fingers push the water over his skin, leaving his chest almost clean, nearly normal. The gray t-shirt I gave Antonio starts helping me wipe, helping me wipe, helping me wipe, catching the drips guided by his tattooed hand.

My fingers fall on the place that is torn open, a slit no wider than a golf ball. Not skin. Flesh. Not sealed. Open. Not flat. Swollen. Not smooth. Edgy. Not mild. Deep. Not red. Black.

My fingers touch the open wound. My head rests on his bare chest. Nothing. No beat from within. My head lifts, but my fingers stay hovering on the cut. My fingers meet death.

No beat. No breath. No one filling this body.

The gray t-shirt still wipes the evidence from his chest, clearing it of the blood that leaves him so altered. My hand stays here, on his chest, my fingers not willing to move just yet. Antonio's distinct hands keep tending to Pedro, I'm sure. I'm sure I see it all around me, but I, I just stay right here, leaning in closer, finding that place where my head rests so perfectly under his chin, and I nestle in once again.

"Pedro, I'm so sorry! I'm so sorry!" I glance at the faces around me, but I can't stop the emotion from pouring out in all the ways I've never allowed it to. I can't keep any of it in. It won't wait. It won't stay inside. It's time to come out. "We didn't have enough time! I needed more time." His neck isn't warm, he doesn't hold me back, his chin doesn't move to the top of my hair, his fingers don't reach for my hair, he doesn't whisper back. He doesn't whisper back. He doesn't whisper back.

Resting there, nestled next to him, I close my eyes. *Father, Why? Why Pedro? Why him?* "Do you know, Pedro? Do you know that I love you?" My tears touch the skin that can't feel anymore. My hair rests on the chest that knows no weight. My words meet the ears that cannot hear. Pressing my lips on his cheek and moving his hair back once again, I shift to my knees. Staring. Staring. At. Him.

"Maggie, Maggie, come here, dear." Marco's gentle voice summons me. I grab hands to stand up, my time coming to a close. My eyes meet his, but they don't see him. They are stuck on the photos they just took. Stuck.

Moments pass and people shift, still huddled around Pedro. Prisoner after prisoner. Friend after friend. Inmate after inmate. Soul after soul. Gathered, they sing. They sing songs we know, songs we've sung, songs he will never sing again.

The sounds of voices fill the space. Mouths are open, and Marco's guitar is being strummed, but my ears don't hear any of it. My mind knows it's happening, but my eyes stare instead of seeing. My heart hurts instead of worshipping. My mind struggles instead of accepting.

Did the Lord put me here just to love and lose this man? Was it me? Is it because I came on Saturday? Did he hurt? Did he know?

The presence of armor cowards from this place, knowing they're the cause this time. The givers of pain can't look at the receivers. They know they aren't safe here today. I know they aren't safe here today. Not this time. Not this crowd. Not our Pedro.

They wait for their safe two o'clock horns to blow, separating the damaged from the damagers, bars securing their safety. Today, the armor is not even safe before this damaged girl.

And I see the line that says you can kill if the conditions are right, the line that values one soul over another. I see the line that says authority is justified, not questioned, the line that says some people are less than others. I see the line that gives them a right, that gives anyone the right, that says who cares, the line that doesn't shed a tear for the one who ended his life in here. I see the line that kills, the line that killed Pedro.

28

still tuesday

A SICKNESS UNLIKE ANY I'VE EVER known came to live within me, weighing me down, leaving me here, planted in this Bronco, too sick to open the door. Too hurt to be a part of life out there. Too hurt to walk inside. Too weak to see a face, to ever see another soul. Too weak to say a prayer.

"Maggie, honey, come on," I'm sure Marco's hand opened the door because I felt him touch my shoulder, but I saw nothing but the dashboard in front of me.

"Maggie..." I'm sure Marco's said something more, but I heard nothing other than my name. In and out, I stared at the dashboard, my stomach cramping, my soul frozen in today. My. Soul. Frozen.

Opening my eyes, I see Marco's light pink house and Victor's subdued face, his hand reaching for mine. Somehow, I manage to walk inside with him.

"Maggie!" Maria runs to me, hugging me tight, I see the black hair next to my eyes, feel her warm touch, and see.

"Ju come here, sweetheart. Ju come and sit." Maria lays my head in her lap, my feet take up the rest of the couch, and there we stay. There we stay, for what seems like hours. Her fingers comb through my hair again and again, occasionally wiping my tears when one would fall.

But mostly I stare, stare at the fabric on the loveseat in front of us, the loveseat. Yes, the loveseat. The one that feels life sit on it daily, the one that absorbs our laughter, that knows our family, that hears the cartoons Diego loves, that comforts our tired bodies and smells our evening popcorn, the one that witnesses our lives. The loveseat, the loveseat that lives.

My eyes can see every line in the fabric, every shade of tan, every hint of thread and each stitch someone sewed. My eyes stare at the loveseat that stares back. It sees me. Right now, it can see me. It can see my blue eyes, the eyes that love him, the eyes that need him, the eyes that don't understand. It sees the stare that says I'm not going to be the same. It can hear the ache of my soul, the "Mmmm" that Maria can't quiet despite her soft touch. It can hear everything. It can see everything. It can feel everything. It hears me suffer. It watches me numb. It feels me lose it all.

Why? Why isn't it Pedro staring back at me? Why aren't *his* eyes looking into mine? Why can't *he* come soothe this ache? Is this really happening? Am I laying here numb because he's never going to be? Never going to hear? Never going to see? Never going to feel? Never going to walk up to me again?

As my mind battles, my chest struggles to breathe, breathing in convulsions, not managing this ache. And even though my Maria holds me tight, my face in her hands, my cries can't be quieted. Can't be quieted.

Can't. Be. Quieted.

I imagine his defined shoulders sitting for the millionth time in their twelve by twelve. The pale peach tiles feeling the bottoms of his feet, the shower wetting his untouched skin, the doors feeling the fingertips that once felt mine…

And life lives beyond the fine line. It lives in every pair of eyes.

CPSIA information can be obtained at www.ICGtesting.com
Printed in the USA
BVOW080339240413

318989BV00001B/51/P